CHOSEN

CHOSEN

Neil Harrison

Illustrated by Dawn Carey Jones

Matador
9 Priory Business Park,
Wistow Road, Kibworth Beauchamp,
Leicestershire. LE8 0RX
Tel: (+44) 116 279 2299
Fax: (+44) 116 279 2277
Email: books@troubador.co.uk
Web: www.troubador.co.uk/matador

ISBN 978 1780881 911

British Library Cataloguing in Publication Data.
A catalogue record for this book is available from the British Library.

Typeset in 11pt Minion Pro by Troubador Publishing Ltd, Leicester, UK

Matador is an imprint of Troubador Publishing Ltd

Printed and bound in the UK by TJ International, Padstow, Cornwall

Josh

CHAPTER 1

Does a good name mean a good person?

When Josh saw the mist changing shape he knew something wasn't right. It shouldn't even have been there. Not on a summer morning anyway.

As the haze shifted around the garden something appeared to form inside it. *That looks like a man* he thought to himself.

A day that should have been bright and yellow was dark and grey. The cool blanket of drizzle drowned the heat of the sun's rays. Two birds, large and black, sat menacingly on the garden fence. This was the second time Josh had seen them. They appeared to be watching him. Not moving. Their silence sent a shiver through Josh.

He flew down the stairs to tell his mum. She was in the kitchen pouring a glass of water and gazing out across the garden.

'Can you see them?' he asked, out of breath.

'See what, love?'

'Look. Over…'

His voice tailed off as he realised that the mist and the birds were no longer there.

'You and your imagination,' she said. 'Always seeing things that aren't there.'

'There were two scary birds and this mist thing. I did, I saw them,' he protested.

His mum kissed him on the forehead and went back to her chair in the lounge. He watched her shuffle away wishing she would get well soon but there was little sign of that happening.

The breeze flitted in through the window and caressed Josh's face. *At least you believe me, don't you?* he thought. His year five visit to the Viking Museum in York had only been a few days ago but he still couldn't get it off his mind. That was the first time he had seen them. And the grey man.

*

It had all started off so well. Inside the museum, the smell of leather, the glint of metal and life-sized models in brown cloaks and grey tunics made everything so real. He first saw the birds on a replica house with their wings spread wide but thought they were just imitation. When he told some of his classmates about them they said they hadn't seen any birds.

The teacher, Mrs Cooper, gave the word and everyone jostled to get on board the special, six-seater electric cars to take them around.

'Steady, steady. Don't forget that this is the site of Jorvik, a real Viking age city, so think about what you're seeing and no silliness when you reach some of the smells,' she said.

The cars passed the scene of a riverfront and arrived at a farmyard. A bitter smell of animals and manure gripped them. Josh's friend, Sam, couldn't resist the temptation and said,

'Pwhoorr! Was that you Keiran?'

Keiran pushed Sam in the back prompting a 'That's enough now!' response from Miss Rothwell, the teaching assistant who was sitting behind them.

As his car edged forward past the statues of the blacksmith and the gossiping lady, Josh sensed the presence of somebody watching them.

The model of a man in a Viking toilet distracted Josh. Everyone laughed and even Miss Rothwell couldn't resist a smile.

'Did you see over there?' Josh elbowed Sam and pointed towards the mock-up of Coppergate Market.

'See what?' replied Sam.

'Someone moved in the shadows at the back.'

'Come on you two, pay attention,' said Miss Rothwell, nodding towards some barking dogs.

When they got out of their cars at the end of the ride, Josh's head was spinning. He tensed up. A blackness crept over him as he looked back to see if he could still see anything unusual. He only started to come out of his hallucination when the group ahead became excited at the holographic Viking ghosts.

'Oh, great! You can see right through them. Can we buy one?' asked Sam.

'I doubt your mum would thank you for taking a Viking ghost back home,' replied Miss Rothwell.

But Josh stopped in his tracks when he saw the last of the five holographic ghosts. It had less colour than the other four and its shape kept changing like a swirling mist. When it stopped moving, the only feature Josh could see was its cloak fastened with a black clasp in the shape of a bird. The figure raised one arm and pointed at Josh with an axe whilst the two large birds sat on his other arm. A chill pierced through him. It would have frozen him to the spot had it not been for Keiran yanking him away.

'Quick! Look at this!' said Keiran dragging Josh towards a cluster of school friends. 'We can make money. Viking coins and stuff.'

He tugged Josh into the huddle. Although some of the chill began to disappear, the image of the figure remained imprinted on Josh's mind.

On the coach back to school Josh sat next to Miss Rothwell.

'You're very quiet, Josh,' she said.

'I was thinking about those ghosts at Jorvik.'

'One's scary enough but four of them…'

'Four?' he asked. 'I saw five.'

'You must be seeing things,' she said.

Miss Rothwell took a museum brochure from her bag and showed Josh the description at the bottom of the page. She read it out to him.

'Our four holographic Viking ghosts will introduce you to.…'

'But there were five. I know,' he interrupted.

'Probably a trick of the light,' said Miss Rothwell.

Josh slumped back in his seat. He spent the rest of the journey back to school arguing in his head between what he saw and the words in the brochure. *Perhaps the brochure was wrong. No. It was the light. But I saw it. Only a trick. He pointed at me. Just imagination. It was real. Couldn't be.*

The squabbling in his head blazed for the rest of the day. Even the responses from his classmates gave no help. Most of the comments from his friends were either 'Dunno' or 'Durr, four thicko.'

Josh ached for someone to believe him.

*

'Josh, could you turn that off for a moment please?' said his mum. I need to talk to you about something.'

'But mum, it's Doctor Who.'

'I know but it's just a repeat and you've seen them all before. This is important.'

'Ohhh!'

Josh's mum leaned forward in her chair and held out her hand to Josh. As she did, a pain shot through her and she winced, gripping the purple cushion that she kept permanently on her lap. Josh scrambled over to her and flung his arms around her neck eager to comfort her.

'Do you want your medicine?' asked Josh wiping the moisture from his eyes that he tried to hide from his mum.

'I've just had some thanks, love. It takes a while to work.'

With one hand she stroked his cheeks and with her other hand ran her fingers through his wavy blond hair. Josh plumped up his mum's cushion to make her more comfortable.

'You know when I went to the hospital last week?' Josh's mum brushed away a tear as she spoke. 'Well they said I've got to have an operation so you'll need to stay with someone else for a while. Just until I'm better.'

Josh felt his heart almost stop beating and he had a sick sensation in his stomach. He asked her about the operation and although his mum tried to explain it, Josh couldn't take it in properly. The only thing that made sense was something having to be taken out because it was bad. Josh fought back the tears, determined not to upset her any more.

If only he had a dad to help. Josh never asked his mum about him because he knew it upset her.

'It'll be all right. I've asked your uncle Nathan and uncle Rupert to come over and talk with us about you staying with one of them. I thought you'd feel better that way.'

'But I want to stay with you.'

Josh knew that would be impossible if his mum was in hospital but he couldn't help wish for it anyway.

'You liked Whitby the last time. You remember your uncles don't you?'

'That was years ago,' said Josh 'and I was with you.'

His mum held him close and felt Josh's heart pounding faster than usual.

'What about my friends?'

'I'm sure you'll make new ones. It's the start of the summer holidays and you'll have some great adventures with them.'

'I've already got friends and I don't want any new ones,' Josh pleaded, slumping back against the side of his mother's chair.

He curled up in a ball and buried his head in his arms trying to block everything out of his mind.

A clap of thunder echoed in the distance dragging him back to reality. His tingling eyes held back more tears like a dam controlling a swelling river. Then a lightning flash illuminated the whole room making everything appear larger and more threatening. The tiger in the painting above the dining table seemed to jump out of the frame. An ornamental bird cast a forbidding shadow against the back wall from its perch on the windowsill. But this was all a trickle compared with the flood in Josh's mind.

Josh ran out of the lounge and clambered up the stairs to his bedroom banging the door shut behind him. The wind chime that hung by the window rustled in the draught. His mum called out after him but the turmoil in his head drowned out her words. He flung himself down on the bed and sank his face into the pillow.

*

On the day that Rupert and Nathan arrived a seashell grey dampness soaked the air. By now, Josh had made up his mind about his uncles although he couldn't recall much about them. Rupert sounded a posh name and maybe he would be very strict. Josh decided that he didn't like him and that uncle Nathan would be more likeable. There was a boy in his class called Nathan and he was very popular. If he had to stay with someone, he would choose Nathan.

Josh poured some orange juice into a jug and made some cheese and marmite sandwiches. They were his favourite.

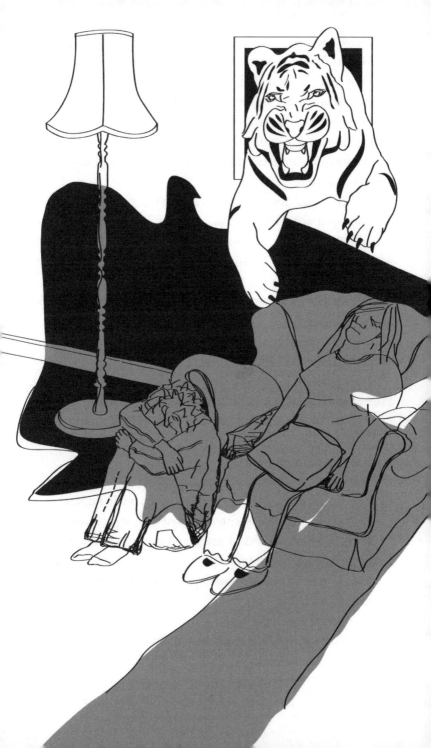

He waited for his uncles to arrive.

His mum was in the armchair sleeping when the bell rang. He went to the front door, looked through the curtain and saw a tall, thin man with long hair and a beard standing outside. The man was wearing a leather jacket and carried a crash helmet under his arm. He smiled but Josh didn't like the look of this bizarre looking stranger so he didn't smile back and closed the curtain instead.

'Mum! Mum!' Josh shouted but there was no reply.

He toyed with the curtain and looked again at the man outside who was still there, smiling. Josh ran back into the lounge and shook his mum. She stirred from her snooze and gradually opened her eyes.

'Mum. There's a man with long hair and a crash helmet. He looks a bit weird.'

'Mmm?…oh it's okay, it'll be Rupert. He always was a bit different. You can let him in.'

Josh went back to the front door. Although his mum had assured him that it would be fine, he was still reluctant to let the man in so he opened it with the chain still on. Josh peered through the crack.

'Are you uncle Rupert?'

'Well that's my name,' the man continued. 'And you are my nephew. So, all in all, I reckon I might just be uncle Rupert.'

Josh stood motionless with a puzzled look on his face.

'Can I come in or shall I just stand in the wet and do sign language through the window?'

Josh wondered how this person could be related to his mum. He seemed odd.

'Mum says you can come in.'

He slid back the door chain and let Rupert in, hoping at the same time that he hadn't just made a big mistake. His uncle towered above him and Josh took a step backwards. Then he slammed the front door shut and hurried to the refuge of his mother.

Rupert strolled into the lounge and gave his frail sister a sympathetic look. She gazed back at him and smiled weakly.

'Hi, sis,' said Rupert in a low tone, his face forcing a smile.

'Do you want a cheese and marmite sandwich?' asked Josh.

'Oh, yes please! Have you tried it with apple?'

Josh screwed up his face in surprise. He had never heard of that before.

'Did you get the newspaper photo I sent you?'

Josh nodded.

The doorbell rang again.

'Answer it will you please, love,' said his mum. 'It'll be Nathan.'

In his eagerness, Josh ran into the hallway to see the uncle he imagined would be terrific.

He opened the door. A short, slightly built man, wearing a dark coat and grey suit, carrying a briefcase, stood outside. Josh smiled at him but the man did not return it. Instead he continued brushing down his coat and adjusting his tie. Eventually he looked up but when he gazed at Josh it was as if the man's eyes were looking straight through him. Josh stared at him for a while, his smile gradually disappearing.

'I'm Nathan. You must be Josh.'

'Yes. Yes I am.'

This wasn't how Josh had imagined him. Nathan strutted into the lounge barely acknowledging his brother and sister. Josh offered him a sandwich.

'Never eat before one o'clock. One of my rules. I never compromise on rules and nor should you.'

'Can't have you breaking a rule, can we Nat?' added Rupert.

'Rules are there for discipline, brother. That's how I got where

I am. And don't call me Nat. It's Nathan.'

Josh sat on the arm of his mother's chair. Nathan brushed the settee with a handkerchief then smoothed down the back of his coat before sitting on the threadbare upholstery. He looked around the room casting occasional stern glances towards his brother. Rupert winked at Josh as he ate two sandwiches with great satisfaction. Josh reached out for his mum who was the only sure thing in a world spiralling into greater uncertainty.

His mum sat up and, smiling, held Josh's hand to reassure him. Nathan glanced at his watch and sighed.

'Still working hard, Nathan?' Josh's mum enquired.

'Of course.'

'And how are you, Rupert?' she added.

'Good thanks. Still working on my dreams. Nobody can take those away.'

'Dreams don't put food on the table,' Nathan continued.

Rupert shrugged his shoulders and pulled a face in Nathan's direction. Josh sniggered, nuzzled closer to his mum and clasped her hand tighter. He knew what Rupert meant about dreams. His mum said if daydreaming was an Olympic sport then Josh would be a gold medal winner. What was wrong with dreams? Except you can't do anything with them. Can you?

'I'm feeling very tired. I'd better explain why I've asked you both to come.' The tone of her voice became more serious. She turned to Josh.

'Would you mind waiting in the kitchen, love? Just for a while.'

Josh didn't move at first but traipsed outside when she touched his arm. He picked up a sandwich as he left.

What is it they don't want me to hear?

Rupert & Nathan

CHAPTER 2

What do you do when a photograph starts changing shape?

Josh brooded on what they were discussing and what was so secret. He tried to eavesdrop but the lounge door was closed and the adults were talking too quietly for him to understand anything. So he sat at the kitchen table and drew moustaches on the cartoons on the side of a packet of cereal. Tears pricked at the back of his eyes and his stomach spun like the washing machine opposite.

Munching his sandwich, he remembered what Rupert had said. Josh took a Golden Delicious apple from the bowl on top of the fridge, bit off a piece and put it in between the half eaten slices of bread. He grinned as the sweetness of the apple mingled with the sourness of the cheese and Marmite. *Wow!* So he bit off some more pieces of apple and placed them in the sandwich.

Josh got bored with doodling and mooched around the kitchen until he stopped by the back door. He surveyed the gloom outside where there should have been summer sun. An odd coloured light, the shade of steel, filled the garden. He looked around for the two birds and the grey man but he couldn't see anything.

*

Rupert called Josh back into the lounge. The adults stared at him as he dawdled in. His future was going to be decided without him having a say in the matter. His body drained of energy and filled up with panic. Josh looked backwards and forwards between the adults trying to work out if their reactions would give a clue to what had been discussed. He chewed his nails as he approached his mother.

'Stop biting your nails! I can't stand that!' snapped Nathan.

Josh waited for his mum's decision. It was like waiting to be chosen for a team at school but not knowing which one you really wanted to be in.

'We've had a good talk, love. We think…perhaps it would be best if you went to stay with uncle Nathan. He's got a lovely house and plenty of room. Lots of places to explore. It shouldn't be for long then I'll be better and we'll be back home again.'

Josh said nothing at first. All he knew was that he didn't want to leave his mum. He just wanted her to get better so they could stay together.

'It's for your own good,' said Nathan.

'How does everyone else know what's best for me? Why doesn't anyone ask me what I want?'

Rupert saw the hurt in Josh's eyes and gently touched Josh's arm.

'I'd love you to stay with me but I've only got this small caravan and your mum thinks it might be a bit cramped.'

Josh wanted to cry but he didn't. He knew it upset his mum.

'Right. That's settled,' said Nathan. 'Put him on the quarter past eleven bus on Monday and I'll meet him at the bus station. It gets in about two thirty. Must go. Business to attend to.'

'Thanks for coming,' said Josh's mum, 'and for all your help.'

'See you, Nat,' muttered Rupert.

'Nathan! It's Nathan!' he complained, pulling the front door shut as he left.

'Anything I can do to help now I'm here?'

Rupert's voice was soft. It seemed like he wanted to help but wasn't sure how. Rupert looked at Josh and smiled but Josh didn't smile back. He was straining to hold back the tears.

'There's nothing, thanks. I know you'd love to have Josh but it wouldn't be fair when you're not earning much.'

Josh saw how much Rupert was trying to help and the early doubts about his quirky uncle began to soften.

'I'll see you later then.'

Rupert hesitated. He was about to say something but stopped himself. Then he left.

As Josh looked through the window, Rupert waved and put his thumb up as if to say everything would be all right. Josh didn't know if that would be the last time he would ever see him.

'I don't want to go!' pleaded Josh.

His mum held out her hand and Josh approached her. She caressed his face and forced a smile, trying to encourage him.

'How come uncle Nathan's got a big house but you and uncle Rupert haven't?'

'He works very hard.'

'What's his job?'

'Some kind of business. I'm not sure exactly. Do you mind, love, I'm a bit tired for questions now. We'll have a long talk about it later. Why don't you go upstairs and think about what you need to take with you? You'll need plenty of clothes so get the big suitcase.'

'When will I come back?'

'As soon as the hospital makes me better.'

'I won't have to change schools will I?'

*

Josh struggled to take the large suitcase down from the top of his wardrobe and thought how he could change the plot of the story unfolding before him. He looked around his room at the newspaper photo Rupert had sent him, the array of posters including Viking longships, clouds and a monkey riding a bike. How long would it be until he saw them again? If ever.

Josh lay on the bed messing about with his Optimus Prime action figure and agonised about the journey to Nathan's.

The wind chime danced and clanged as he stared again at the newspaper photo of the Viking festival. It began to change in front of him. The previously hazy figure in a cloak began to move and pointed an axe at him. *Like at the Viking museum.* Josh sat up, startled. He rubbed his eyes to check if he was imagining it.

He wasn't.

CHAPTER 3

How do you feel when the unexpected happens?

Josh finished packing. He had all the clothes he thought he would need and some special possessions including a book on Vikings and the wind chime that his granddad had sent him when he was a baby. It was coloured gold, in the shape of a fairground carousel with children riding clouds instead of horses. One of the clouds had a piece missing but it was Josh's favourite cloud because he thought it looked like a sloth. Sloths fascinated Josh because they moved very slowly and could hang upside down when they slept. Josh tried it himself once but he became dizzy and didn't do it again.

He loved his wind chime. It told him when his friend, the breeze, was around. Even if he couldn't see or touch his friend, the wind chime would make him aware of his presence. Josh called it a him because it seemed like a father would be; always there watching over him, even when you couldn't see him.

Josh considered taking his large wall map of the world with him but decided not to. He had put pins in all the places his dreams had carried him and he thought removing all the pins would destroy everything. He wanted to keep something normal in his room amidst all the upheaval. Leaving the map gave him hope that he would soon return and continue his travels and dreaming. At the last minute he remembered the mobile phone that his mum had bought him last Christmas but which he seldom used.

It was almost ten o'clock when Josh dragged his suitcase down the stairs to the front door. His mother was still in bed. She rarely got up before midday because she needed her rest. Josh made her a cup of tea and some toast the way she liked it; thinly spread marmalade without any margarine. His mum was stirring when he carried the tray into her room and placed it by the bed. She gazed at him through bleary eyes.

'I'll try and get up to see you off, love. Really I will. Mrs Kendrick will be round soon and she knows exactly where to go for the bus. I'm going to miss you so much.'

Josh kissed and hugged her. She held her face against his and stroked his neck where his birthmark was. A birthmark that appeared more noticeable since the news that he had to leave home. He didn't want to let her go but a glimpse of the clock on the bedside table forced him from her.

Josh went downstairs and waited in the kitchen for his next-door neighbour, Mrs Kendrick, to drive him to the bus station. His mum had written down the number of the bus he had to catch. Clutching the note and his bus fare, he sat alone watching the clock hands cruelly tugging him towards the time that he hoped would never come. He wanted to stop time but it was out of his control.

At ten thirty Mrs Kendrick knocked on the back door and Josh let her in.

'All ready then?'

'I want to say goodbye to mum.'

'Better leave her, dear,' replied Mrs Kendrick. 'I'm sure she'll phone you later when you get to your uncle's. Come on, we don't want to be late.'

Looking around the hall and into the lounge, he noticed the photo of him and his mum taken at the seaside. That was when he was much younger and his mum wasn't sick. He grabbed the photo and put it inside his rucksack with some sandwiches and a bottle of water.

He gazed at the upstairs landing hoping his mum had managed to get up early to see him off as she said but it was silent.

'Bye mum!' Josh called out more in hope than expectation. He looked around and breathed in the scent of home as if to capture it for future recall.

Josh followed Mrs Kendrick to her car. Together they heaved his suitcase into the car boot then he sat in the front seat, his stomach tightening with every second that passed. As they pulled away, he looked up at the window where his mum was waving at him. Josh wound down the window and waved back at her. The breeze dried a tear that had tried to escape and he wondered if he would ever run out of that front door to school again.

Driving past his school, Josh thought about his friends who were enjoying the start of the summer holidays. Holidays that seemed to go on forever. He stared out of the window at the familiar parts of Leeds which passed by like a speeded up film and which he would not see for…how long? He held back the flood of tears. *Don't cry*. That was a rule he set himself. One with which uncle Nathan would surely agree. Josh gripped his rucksack, desperate to cling on to something familiar.

*

After nearly two hours on the bus, mainly spent playing Snake on his mobile phone, Josh opened the packet of marmalade sandwiches he had made earlier.

As the bus turned off the main road, leaving behind the wilderness of the moors, he caught sight of the signpost. Goathland. He thought the name sounded fantastic and mystical, like a made up name from a book or a film and wondered if there were such things as Goaths.

Down the road for several minutes then the bus slowed and

turned right past an old church. Mist swirled eerily around the graveyard in a ghostly dance and changed shape as it moved. Two large birds watched the bus from their perch on one of the gravestones. *It's them. Like in the garden.* He thought he had left them behind. Heaviness crept over Josh.

A few minutes later, the bus drew to a halt at a small bus shelter that looked like a miniature house with a red tiled roof and white wooden gate. Opposite was a row of shops and a cafe.

'Quick rest stop,' the driver announced. 'All right, son?' he continued, looking at Josh.

Josh nodded back at the driver who got out of the bus then jogged over to the cafe and disappeared inside.

Josh was still thinking about the birds and the mist in the graveyard when he glimpsed a man wearing a crash helmet sitting inside the bus shelter. Because of the angle he couldn't see the man clearly. Josh took out his book to read and paid him no more attention. Moments later, the man emerged from the bus shelter and stood outside the bus looking up at him. Josh saw him out of the corner of his eye but dared not look straight at him. The man didn't move. Finally, when Josh did turn towards him he nearly choked on his sandwich.

The man removed his crash helmet and bobbed his head inside the bus.

'Uncle Rupert!'

'Hi ya.'

'What are you doing here?' exclaimed Josh with a mixture of surprise and unease. Just as he thought nothing more surprising could happen, Josh was flung into even greater confusion.

'Come on, we're going to my place. I can't have you stopping with Nathan. It'll be like a prison.'

'But mum's expecting me to go.'

'I'll phone her later. Where's your case?'

'It's in the luggage bit at the side but the driver's got to open it. I don't know if I should.'

'Don't worry, I'll tell the driver. Pass me your rucksack.'

Josh thought twice but then gathered his possessions.

He was getting off the bus as the driver returned with a cup of coffee.

'Excuse me, mate,' said Rupert. 'Can we get his suitcase out? He's getting off here.'

'He said he was going to Whitby.'

'Yeah. Change of plan,' said Rupert.

'Do you know this man?'

'He's my uncle Rupert.'

The driver looked questioningly at Rupert and was unsure whether he should let Josh go or not.

'Look, I know you're only being careful and I'm grateful. Here's his mum's phone number,' said Rupert. 'Call her if you're worried.'

Josh offered to phone on his mobile but when he tried, all he got was a *NO SIGNAL* message.

'That all right by you, son?'

Josh glanced back and forth between the two men then nodded to the driver. He didn't know if he was doing the right thing and if his mum would be angry.

The driver opened the luggage compartment and took out Josh's suitcase. Rupert took it and led Josh away from the bus to a motorbike parked by the cafe. Josh looked in bewilderment at the gleaming two-wheeled machine with a large box behind the passenger seat. Rupert took a crash helmet from the box and placed it on Josh's head. The helmet was too big for Josh and Rupert struggled to contain a laugh as he adjusted it so he could still see through it. Rupert helped Josh put his rucksack on his back.

'My case! What about my case?' blurted out Josh.

Rupert smiled that smile he gave Josh at his mum's house when he first met him.

'No problem. Mountain will get it.'

'Mountain?'

Just as Rupert spoke, Josh was startled by the largest man he had ever seen coming out of the cafe eating a meat pie. The man strode towards him and picked up his suitcase with one hand as he continued eating. Josh took a backward step.

'Uncle Rupert! Uncle Rupert!' exclaimed Josh.

'Feeding your face again, eh Mountain? Josh, this is my buddy Mountain.'

Mountain waved a half chewed meat pie at Josh and gave him a closed-mouth grin.

'Big isn't he?' said Rupert as Mountain juggled Josh's suitcase like it was a small, soft toy.

'How did he get so big?'

'His mum used to put manure in his shoes.'

Josh looked wide-eyed and open-jawed at Rupert.

'No. Not really.' Rupert paused then continued. 'She put it in his socks.'

'Oh,' said Josh, not knowing whether Rupert was joking or serious.

Rupert helped Josh clamber onto the passenger seat of the motorbike before getting on himself.

'Hold tight round my waist. I won't go too fast.'

'But my case.' Josh was still anxious about his belongings and the change of plan.

'Mountain's got a bigger bike. He'll strap it on the back with his fishing gear and meet us at my place.'

Rupert started up the motorbike and they accelerated away from the cafe. Past the garage with its bright blue doors, over a railway line then up the hill onto the open moors. Josh felt the breeze sweeping over him. The breeze encouraged him. Never left him. A friend. Constant.

They followed the snaking road across the moors; a vast expanse of treeless countryside like Josh had never seen before. He wanted to ask where they were going but the speed took his breath away and it was all he could do to hold on to Rupert's waist. Josh began to think that Rupert lived in the middle of nowhere.

As they descended a steep hill towards a village, Rupert slowed the bike down. He turned round to Josh and tapped him on his arm to reassure him as they waited at traffic lights. Josh was still anxious about his suitcase. He couldn't see Mountain.

'Not far now. About ten minutes,' mumbled Rupert from underneath his crash helmet.

Up the other side of the hill and onto higher ground, Josh noticed words on road signs that made him doubt his earlier thoughts about the location of Rupert's caravan. Bay. Marina. Regatta. The smells, sights and sounds were vaguely familiar and awoke a slumbering memory. Fish. Salt. Seagulls. Children carrying small fishing nets. The glimpse of a boat's mast. Then more masts.

Crossing a bridge over a river, Josh looked to his left and saw a lighthouse at the river mouth. His stomach somersaulted. Was that the lighthouse from the holiday with his mum several years ago? Josh's excitement was so great he almost forgot he was on the back of a motorbike. He started to take one of his arms from around Rupert's waist but Rupert felt the softening of pressure around him and moved Josh's arm firmly back.

'Keep tight,' shouted Rupert over the noise of the engine and the crowded pavements.

From the bridge, Rupert turned left up a small cobbled street. Through the gaps between the houses and shops, Josh could see the river. He couldn't take his eyes off it. Rupert drove at walking pace through the clusters of people flitting like wasps between the shops. As the road climbed so did Josh's hope. Hope that this was the place he had visited before and whose recollections were stirring. Yet as his confidence increased so did his doubts. He still didn't know why Rupert had brought him here. They would both have a lot of explaining to do to his mum and uncle Nathan.

The memory of the birds and the grey mist at Goathland sprung back into his mind.

With Josh's thoughts still fizzling in his head, the road narrowed and became as steep as a playground slide. Rupert told Josh to hang on tighter. It was only a short climb but the motorbike was straining by the time they reached the top.

The road levelled off again and they were out in the open, away from the bustle, passing an old church on the cliff top with tombstones arranged like sponge fingers in a trifle. On the other side of the road was a much bigger, even older looking church with no roof and crumbling walls where the windows had long since disappeared. *Who'd be interested in that old ruin?* What he didn't realise was that, one day, this rundown building would hold his future.

A few hundred metres later they turned left by a small post box through a gate in a crumbling Yorkshire stone wall. A long road through open fields guided them towards the sea and a park with rows of individual caravans but unlike any he had seen before. Rupert stopped at the furthest one that was set on higher ground with views of the sea in one direction and the park shop, café and a playground in the other.

Josh dismounted, his crash helmet lopsided over his eyes. Rupert's smile broke into a laugh.

'What a state. You look as if you've just been fired from a cannon.'

The caravan, which was bigger than Josh expected, was painted white and raised off the ground on concrete blocks. Steps led up to a green wooden balcony that surrounded the caravan on two sides. Josh glanced around the rest of the caravan park and started to panic.

'My case. Where's my case?'

Banjo

CHAPTER 4

What makes a home?

Just as he spoke, Josh heard the throaty drone of another motorbike. Mountain pulled up with Josh's case. He unhitched it taking care not to damage the fishing rod strapped on the side. Then, taking what was left of his meat pie from a compartment on the back of his bike, he stuffed it in his mouth and carried the case on his shoulder up the steps into the caravan. Josh watched him with a mixture of disbelief and amazement. Mountain emerged several moments later.

'Cheers, buddy. I owe you one. Catch you at the café later,' said Rupert following Mountain out of the caravan.

Giving a thumbs up sign to Rupert, Mountain then punched the air in a victory gesture to Josh.

He had only met Mountain twice but he had still not heard him speak. Mountain rode off through the gate until the hum of his motorbike faded to nothing.

'Good guy that Mountain,' said Rupert. 'Coming in?'

'Mum said you lived in a caravan.'

'It's a static one. Not the sort you tow behind cars. All right isn't it? Best go and ring Nathan and your mum. I'll ask Annie in the office if I can use her phone.'

Josh offered the use of his mobile phone but Rupert said it would be too expensive. He was going to have a lot of explaining to do.

'Nathan will be waiting at the bus station,' Rupert continued 'and he's going to have a right mood on. Bet this isn't in his rulebook. There's orange in the fridge and biscuits in the jar. Will you be all right on your own for a bit?'

Josh nodded. He glanced around and wondered if staying with uncle Rupert might be better than being with uncle Nathan. He questioned whether it was right to feel good about something even if it was going against someone's wishes. He hadn't hurt anybody; that wasn't in his nature. *I haven't lied to anyone or stolen anything.* Josh hoped that uncle Rupert phoning his mum and uncle Nathan to tell them where he was would make things all right.

Josh explored the caravan. There was a small kitchen on one side with a fixed, round dining table and cushioned seating around two sides of the table. The seating continued through to a lounge area at the end of the caravan with large windows looking out on three sides. Pictures of the sea and the ruined building they had passed earlier hung on the walls. The TV in the corner was one of the smallest he had seen. A jumble of motorbike magazines lay on a low table in the middle of the lounge alongside an empty blue mug with the words 'Biker Dude' on the side and an empty packet of custard cream biscuits. At one end of the caravan there were some closed doors. He sniffed the air. *Marmite.* Josh grinned.

He knelt on the cushions by the biggest of the three windows and looked out beyond a grassy area to the cliff and the sea. To the left, he could just make out the top of the lighthouse behind the ruins. On the right were other fixed caravans and then a stone wall beyond which he couldn't see. The more he gazed at the sea the more the knots in his stomach untangled.

As Josh studied the pictures on the wall there was a knock at the door.

'Hey, Rupert! You in there, man?'

The voice was deep. A man's voice. He wondered if it might

be Mountain. He wasn't sure because he had never heard him speak.

'Yo!'

The voice became more forceful. Josh crouched down on the floor.

'I'm mad! Really mad!' the voice went on.

Josh breathed slowly in case he could be heard but his pulse was racing so much that he had to gulp in air. Beads of sweat blossomed on his forehead. His stomach tightened again. Mouth dry. But the growing panic dissolved when Josh heard another voice. One he recognised.

'I'm really sorry, Banjo mate. Completely forgot. You'd better come in.'

'Half hour, man. Half hour. It's like a disastrophy.'

'Want you to meet someone.'

'We're late for my gig. Like, late late.'

'Josh! Josh?'

Getting up from the floor, Josh gave an embarrassed, half-hearted grin. He stared in disbelief at the eccentric character alongside Rupert. Banjo was short, stick thin and wore a dark blue and white striped bandanna on his head. An untidy beard sprouted across his face and his uneven and different shaped teeth appeared as if they had been put into his mouth at random by somebody blindfolded.

'You lost something?' said Rupert.

Josh looked around the room trying to get some inspiration for what to say.

'Errm…a marble.'

'Love marbles. Got any good 'uns?' said Banjo.

'You lost your marbles yonks ago. Josh, this is my mate Banjo.'

'Yo bro!'

'Pardon?' said Josh.

'Granted.'

Banjo held out his hand for a high five but Josh hesitated before returning the gesture. Banjo then moon-walked round the room humming whilst Josh looked on in disbelief at the scarecrow-like man who seemed lost in his own world. Rupert rolled his eyes and shook his head.

'Sorry about the mess up, Banjo. How about I buy you breakfast tomorrow?' Banjo's face lit up at the mention of food.

'Fantastico. High five!' Banjo held out his hand again to Josh. This time Josh was more prepared. Banjo left humming a tune and playing air guitar.

'I've spoken to your mum and Nathan.'

Josh sat down and gripped a cushion tight, bracing himself for the worst.

'Phew, got my ear well chewed off. I said I'd like you to stay here. Like a sort of holiday. Your mum said it's all right for a while but she still wants you to go to Nathan's later. What do you think?'

Josh didn't reply immediately. He wasn't used to people asking him what he wanted or how he felt. He didn't know what to say.

'What feels right for you, Josh? Say how you feel.'

Josh looked out of the window at the top of the lighthouse then round to the sea and the horizon beyond. After a while, his face softened into a broad grin.

'It feels…good. Is it okay to stay?'

'It would be great. But don't go pinching Rover's biscuits.'

Josh's eyes widened and he sat up straight.

'You've got a dog?'

Rupert shook his head. Josh looked puzzled and screwed up his nose.

'He's a cat but I call him Rover 'cos he's always disappearing. Goes off for days sometimes. Then comes back when he feels like it. Want to check out your bedroom?'

Josh's room had a single bed, a white bedside table and a small table lamp with a faded orange lampshade. A brown coloured photograph of an old sailing ship hung on the wall. A built in wardrobe with a mirror on the outside filled one end of the room. The window faced out towards the lighthouse.

'You okay with the lighthouse shining through your window at night?' asked Rupert.

'It'd be good. Like it's protecting me as well as the ships.'

Sitting on the bed, Josh gazed out of the window. Rupert sat next to him. In silence they watched seagulls swoop and glide above the cliff.

'Great isn't it?'

Josh looked up at Rupert and nodded although he wished that his mum was there with him. He leaned against Rupert and savoured the calm that washed over him soothing away the ache that had gripped him for the last few days.

'It's going to be all right,' Rupert reassured him. 'You sort yourself out. When you're ready you can help me deliver some stuff round town.'

'What sort of stuff?'

'I'm a motorbike courier. I take letters and parcels between shops and offices when people want something delivered quickly. Soon as we've finished we'll go to the cafe.'

Josh played with the pillow, wondering why it appeared as if Rupert had been expecting him.

'Uncle Rupert?'

'Just call me Rupert. Uncle sounds old.'

'Okay. This is…Whitby isn't it?'

'Certainly is. Captain Cook. Dracula. Ghosts and vampires. And that's just Banjo's house.'

Rupert winked at Josh who belatedly realised the joke and smirked at the thought.

'And what's that old place like a church with no walls or anything?'

'Oh, the abbey? It's nearly a thousand years old. I used to play there loads when I was your age.'

'Rupert?'

'Yeah?'

'Why did you come for me at Goathland?'

Rupert paused.

'Maybe we'll talk about it later, eh?'

Josh knew that when adults said 'later', it usually meant they wanted to avoid the subject because there was something difficult to explain. As he looked out of the window towards the lighthouse gleaming in the afternoon sunshine, Josh wondered what was holding Rupert back.

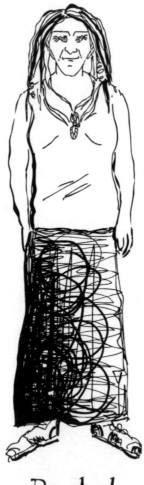

Rachel

CHAPTER 5

When does a sign become a danger sign?

Josh unpacked and hung up his wind chime. His friend breathed through the window causing the chime to ring and the clouds on the wind catcher to whirl. He smiled, reassured that his old friend hadn't deserted him. He propped up his photo against the window so his mum could see the lighthouse. He kissed her and told her his thoughts as if she was there with him. This wasn't Josh's home but somehow, putting all his things out made it feel a bit like home.

*

It took Josh and Rupert an hour and a half to deliver the parcels, largely because Rupert had spent a lot of time talking to a lady at a spooky museum down by the harbour. She was dressed in a style he had never seen before. Dark make-up and a long black dress with gloves half way up her arms. She kissed Rupert as he left and waved at Josh.

'Who was that?' asked Josh.

'That's my girlfriend, Mina. I've told her all about you. She's offered to show you round town tomorrow so you'll meet her then. Only if you want that is.'

'What were those funny clothes she was wearing?'

'She'll tell you tomorrow. Come on, let's eat.'

They drove a short way up a winding road to a café with views across the sea. Several motorbikes were parked outside. Rupert led them in.

'Ruby, this is my nephew Josh,' said Rupert to a woman, almost hidden behind a counter piled high with cakes, buns and bottles of fruit juice.

Mountain sat at a table nearest the counter with a large mug of tea, tucking into an enormous plate of sausages, mashed potato and peas. He gave his familiar salute. Banjo playfully threw a crumpled paper napkin in Rupert's direction but it narrowly missed him and landed in a lady's tea.

'Soz, Rachel. Meant for Rupert,' Banjo apologised.

The lady, who wore a white sleeveless top and long blue patterned skirt, remained seated. She gave Banjo such a piercing look that he scurried out of the café.

'Oohhhh, not that look again!' Banjo shouted as he dashed outside.

Josh thought he saw her eyes glow but he blinked hard and dismissed the idea.

Everyone in the café laughed whilst Josh looked on open-mouthed.

'Sorry love, didn't mean to worry you. I'm Rachel.'

She wiped the remnants of a cream bun from her fingers and beamed at Josh. His face relaxed and he smiled back at her. Rachel was a similar age to his mum with fair hair that flowed down to her shoulders. It was the brightness of her eyes that captivated him the most. There was something about Rachel that made Josh think he knew her.

'I've been looking forward to seeing you,' she said.

Her words made Josh flinch. *How could she be? She doesn't know me.*

Ruby took an enormous jam doughnut from one of the displays on her counter.

'Got a rule for new customers in this café,' she declared.

She sounded serious but the twinkle in her eye betrayed the words.

'Ruby's famous doughnut dare,' she continued. 'You have to eat the giant doughnut in three minutes without licking your lips. If you can't finish it, you never set foot in my café again.'

'Go on Josh lad. Best shot,' said Rachel.

Banjo sneaked back into the café to watch Josh attacking the doughnut as if his whole future depended on it. He had eaten half of it when he noticed that everyone in the café was gathering around him. They started chanting in unison.

'Josh! Josh! Josh! Josh!'

They repeated his name quicker and quicker whilst Josh ate in time with their chorus until he had finished the whole doughnut without licking his lips.

'One minute forty nine seconds,' announced Ruby.

'Must be a record,' said Rachel.

Josh grinned a jammy grin and looked at Rupert who held his arms aloft in a victory celebration. People were cheering him and Mountain punched the air repeatedly to acknowledge the achievement. Josh couldn't remember if he had ever felt better.

Ruby shouted across the cafe.

'Rupert. Phone.'

A huddle gathered around Josh. A few minutes earlier these people were unknown to him but now they were patting him on the back and congratulating him like real friends. When Rupert came back he was writing something in a notebook.

'Sorry, Josh. I've got to pick up a parcel and take it to Scarborough. Might not be back 'til late.' Rupert turned to Rachel.

'Couldn't stop with Josh could you Rachel?'

Rachel apologised, explaining that she had to go out of town to have a new exhaust fitted on her motorbike. Rupert asked some other people but they couldn't help. Suddenly Josh felt a hand on his shoulder and a voice singing.

'Heeeyyy yaaaaa. I'm the man. I'm the man,' Banjo warbled, dancing on the spot.

'Last time you helped me you lost a parcel at Flamingo Land Zoo,' said Rupert.

'Hey, chill! Not my fault the giraffes were hungry. Anyway you owe me, right?'

Rupert scratched his head.

'Okay. But no crazy stuff!'

'Me? I may be mad but I'm not crazy. Safety central me.'

Rupert wasn't convinced by Banjo's claims but he didn't have many options left. He glanced around the room looking for alternatives but nothing surfaced.

'No messing about. I'm warning you.'

'Fabulicious!' Banjo enthused.

'Bring Josh back to my place about eight o'clock. No later.'

'Done,' said Banjo.

'You will be if you don't get back in time,' replied Rupert. 'Better go. Catch you back at the caravan at eight.'

Josh nodded hesitantly. Rupert left the café and waved to him as he drove off on his motorbike in the direction of the harbour.

'Any problems with wacko here, you let me know,' said Rachel.

Her words had a protective quality about them. Yet it was still her eyes that struck him most. As he gazed at her, he began to see someone much older but who still looked young. As if she had lived a thousand years but never aged. *That's impossible.* The notion scared him. Excited him.

*

Banjo danced out of the café and down the hill. Josh followed at

40

a distance, the doubt creeping back in the further he moved away from the café.

'Ever been on a quad bike, Josho?'

'What's a quad bike?'

'It's like major fun!'

Down by the beach, Banjo unlocked the door of a bright red hut and wheeled out what looked like a motorbike on four fat tyres. Banjo gave Josh a crash helmet then started the engine as Josh squeezed onto the saddle behind him. Like the one Rupert had given him for the ride to Whitby, the helmet was way too big.

'We have lift off,' shrieked Banjo.

They edged down the steep concrete slipway then accelerated along the beach that was almost deserted. A squall had picked up and rain drifted in from the sea. Josh felt the dampness whirling around, stinging his face. Banjo yelled with delight as he steered the quad bike along the shoreline spraying foam over them and soaking their legs.

With Rupert, Josh had felt enlivened but safe. But with Banjo things felt less certain as the weather deteriorated. They sped back and forth along the shoreline for a while then turned out towards a sandbank about fifty metres from shore but still navigable on dry land. Banjo stopped the bike on the sandbank and dismounted.

'What you think, Joshy? Mad eh?'

'Shouldn't we get back?'

'Plenty time.'

Josh's uneasiness rose as the sky darkened and the waves around the sandbank swelled. He studied the menacing steel grey sky heavy with puffy clouds rising vertically. A mist, previously far out at sea, intensified as it lurched towards them. What seemed like a ghost ship with sails and dragon headed bow took shape from the depths of the haze. He thought he saw the outline of a warrior from bygone times wielding a sword and shield. Closing his eyes, he tried to erase the image from his head. *Can't be.*

Head pounding. Heart thumping. Stomach twisting. Josh cringed when Banjo shouted out,

'Power of nature, eh?'

An unseen conductor stirred up the waves like an orchestra.

'Can we go now? Please?' Josh begged.

'Okay. But you're missing the party.'

Josh leapt on the quad bike so quickly that he would have driven off without Banjo if he had known how to start it. Banjo tried to persuade the machine into life but a wave hit the sand bank and drenched it. He tried several times to get it going but failed. The invading tide was now covering the sandbank. Josh trembled and Banjo's bravado ebbed away as fast as the sea covered their tiny island.

'Better leave it. Have to wade back.'

Banjo looked around but the route they had taken was engulfed with water.

The sky was a dark, spinning canopy of cloud, wind and rain. Josh had never seen weather like this. Banjo had been so caught up with his dash for excitement that he had ignored the danger signs. Gathering in strength, the storm howled around them chilling their wet skin.

'What shall we do?' Josh pleaded, his voice weakening.

Josh thought of his mum. She wanted him to go to Nathan's. *Perhaps she was right.* Boring and too many rules suddenly looked appealing. For the first time since Rupert had met him in Goathland, Josh wished that Rupert had not been so bothered about him. Was that wrong? Thoughts crashed into his head, all competing for attention and demanding they be heard. Everything moved so fast and out of control. Josh's pulse galloped.

His breath became shallower. Images of Rachel sprinted through his head but he didn't know why.

'You swim?' Banjo's voice echoed with worry. 'Just in case.'

'I can't,' revealed Josh, tears welling up in his eyes that he fought back.

'Okay, we're cool.'

Banjo put his arm around Josh. He tossed aside their crash helmets that thrashed about in the swirling water before disappearing.

'Stick together. Ready?'

Josh said nothing. His only reply was to grip Banjo's arm tighter than ever as they took a few cautious steps in the direction of the shore. Their only dry haven had slipped deeper under the water with Josh's legs now covered by foaming sea to just below his knees.

They took another step and felt their feet give way. Josh almost slipped under the water but Banjo managed to catch him.

'Try another way,' yelled Banjo.

The tide was coming in so quickly that they could barely tell where the sandbank had been. The quad bike was swamped. Josh wanted to believe they would be okay but his hope was fading. He didn't know who was holding who tightest as Banjo clutched him closer.

Banjo looked down at Josh.

'We're good,' said Banjo with little conviction.

A fearful cold stifled Josh's voice. The sea encroached further.

'Hold round my neck,' screamed Banjo. 'Not too tight.'

Banjo stooped down and Josh climbed onto his back.

'Hold on and close your mouth.'

Banjo staggered towards the shore. The water came up to his knees and rose with every step. When the water reached chest level he started to swim. The first strokes were easy and they seemed to be making headway. Then a large wave hit them and forced them both under the water. Josh pulled on Banjo's neck and kicked down with his feet just as Banjo grasped Josh's coat and lifted them both above the surface sufficient to gasp some air. Neither of them could speak. Josh held onto Banjo's collar with one hand and made paddling movements with the other.

As the waves thrashed around, Josh again caught sight of the warrior and the dragon ship. So near.

The storm increased. All they could think of was surviving. Though the tide was coming in fast, a current seemed to be dragging them out to sea and the shore looked further away from them. Josh put so much effort into paddling that it made him lose his grip. The next wave hit them from behind with such force that he became separated from Banjo and was flung around like a sock in a washing machine. It left him face up in the sea, struggling to breathe but desperately trying not to swallow any water. He gulped more air into his stretched lungs.

Josh wanted to call out but he needed all his strength to keep afloat. He flailed around in the sea but within seconds a gigantic wave lifted him up and hurled him through the frothing waters. Images sprinted through his mind. It was like watching a high-speed train rushing before him. Each compartment containing an event in his life or the face of somebody he had known.

Then everything went dark.

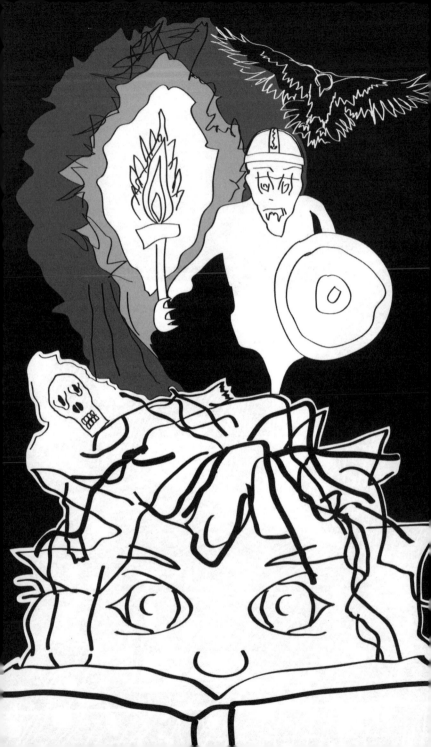

CHAPTER 6

If something looks strange is it always dangerous?

The next thing Josh knew, he was onshore with his face down in a mush of sand and foam. Thinking he was still in the sea, he started to paddle wildly. When he opened his eyes he saw he had been thrown onto the beach. He spat the gritty water from his mouth and spluttered Banjo's name. Looking in front and to his left he couldn't see him. As he came round, he felt something pull him sharply upwards.

'You good, Joshy boy?'

Josh recognised Banjo's voice, turned round and clung on to him as the rain lashed down and the tide thrashed angrily around their legs.

'Those waves,' said Banjo. 'Couldn't see you. Come on, Rachel lives over there.'

Josh looked back at the furious waves and glimpsed the outline of the warrior standing in the surf. He pointed his sword directly at Josh then turned and walked back through the breakers until the mist shrouded him from view. Banjo didn't seem to notice.

They turned their backs on the sea and stumbled towards some steps. On the cliff top Josh saw a woman with long fair hair and a billowing cloak looking down at them. She vanished when she saw them reach the steps, out of reach of the raging sea. *Who was that?*

*

'Come on, get yourselves in here.'

Rachel took them into the lounge of her small fisherman's cottage by the pier. She fetched towels and put the kettle on for a hot drink but didn't appear surprised to see them.

'Maximum regret, Josho. Shouldn't have done it.'

Josh didn't know what to say. He held Banjo's arm to reassure him even though his head and body were churning. Banjo reached out and held him tight. Rachel came back into the lounge but stopped by the door when she saw the two of them clasping each other.

When they finally let each other go Rachel pretended not to notice and gave them their towels.

'Lucky you caught me in. Wallies got the wrong exhaust. Came back early I did.'

They all sat in silence for a while although Banjo couldn't stand it for long.

'Want to know what happened?' he asked.

Rachel didn't say anything but continued drying Josh's hair. He didn't expect her reaction. *Why doesn't she ask?*

Banjo explained what they had gone through. Josh sat quietly at first but had to say something eventually.

'He didn't mean it. The storm came in so quickly.'

'You don't mess with the sea,' said Rachel. 'You especially, Banjo, should know that. Didn't you see the storm signs?'

Rachel beamed at Josh like she had done at the café earlier. Josh ran up and held her tight.

'You're all right, love,' said Rachel. 'You're all right.'

He thought about the warrior in the storm and wanted to tell Rachel.

'I saw something on the beach.'

She kissed his head and held the towel tightly around him, drawing him closer to her. As she wiped Josh's hair away from his eyes she noticed a birthmark on his neck. She tensed up. Josh sensed the change and looked up at her.

'Is something wrong?' he asked.

'No, love. Just thinking.' She paused a while and nuzzled Josh's hair. 'Everything's fine.'

Banjo also noticed the change in her but, for once, remained quiet. The look in Rachel's eyes unnerved him. It reminded him of the time he'd seen her in the abbey grounds one evening, on her knees as if praying. She was with several other women in a similar pose. But it wasn't what they appeared to be doing that terrified him. It was that their eyes glowed and a gleaming light surrounded them.

Banjo closed his eyes, looked down at the floor and covered himself in his towel.

'Someone was looking after you, no mistake,' said Rachel.

'Banjo you mean?' asked Josh.

'Somebody bigger.'

'Who?'

'Just remember.' Rachel held Josh's face in her hands. 'Hot chocolate. Then we'll work out what to tell Rupert.'

*

Rupert arrived back home just before eight o'clock. There was no sign of Josh or Banjo as he drove up to his front door and went inside. He made a cup of tea and sat on the doorstep staring at the gate.

Waiting.

The rain had stopped and the clouds handed over the sky to

a coral tinged setting sun. A smell of damp grass hung in the air. Rupert's anxiety increased as it got to nearly half past eight. He couldn't wait any longer and locked his front door before driving off to Banjo's house.

As he arrived at the small cottage Banjo shared with his mother, his misgivings at leaving Josh deepened. Rupert knocked several times before Banjo's mother opened the door.

'Sorry to bother you, Mrs Waters. Not seen Banjo have you?'

'Oh, come in, dear,' she said, patting her hearing aid. 'I've just made some tea.'

'Sorry but I'm in a real hurry. Has Banjo got back?'

'Banjo's got a yak? Where's he going to keep it?'

'Don't worry. Thanks anyway. See you later.'

Rupert sped off, only just avoiding the dustbins at the side of the road. His mind was in a whirl and he didn't know who to contact next. He thought of other people at the café who Banjo may have taken Josh to see. Rachel's name leapt into his mind but she said she wouldn't be back 'til late. Where else? His pulse raced. Maybe the club where Banjo often played with his band? But that was in the next village. It would take too long to get there.

Rupert stopped to think about where he could go. Who? He scrolled through names in his head but nobody in particular jumped out at him. He wished he'd got round to replacing his lost mobile phone earlier but it was too late now. Somebody. There must be somebody. Ruby? No she would still be clearing up after closing and she would have phoned Annie at the caravan park office to leave a message. Names. Places. They all jumped through Rupert's head but they were all confusion.

'Think! Stop and think! Where else? Who might know?' he said aloud, trying to sort out his ideas.

Even though Rachel said she would not be at home, something led Rupert to go to her house. He drove manically through the side streets and was lucky there were few people around.

He pulled up outside Rachel's whitewashed cottage and knocked so hard he grazed his knuckles on the coarse wood door.

'Rachel! Rachel! You there?'

Rupert turned away and started to remount his motorbike when the door opened.

'Hey! Didn't think you'd be in.'

'That why you knocked? He's inside and he's all right so don't get in a beef.'

Rupert dashed into the lounge where Josh and Banjo, wrapped in blankets, were sipping hot chocolate.

'Are you all right?' said Rupert running over to Josh. 'You're soaking. What happened?'

'I'm okay. Honest.'

Banjo rose timidly from his chair.

'Like, soz man.'

Rachel could see Rupert was about to explode.

'Sit. Let them explain before you blow up.' She took hold of Rupert's shoulders and directed him to a chair by the window.

'There better be a good explanation for this 'cos if…'

'Less talking, more listening, right? Go on then,' she prompted Banjo.

His eyes flicked everywhere except directly at Rupert. Banjo recounted the whole episode and Josh chipped in now and then. Rupert tried to get a word in but when he did Rachel gave him a stern look. Realising how hard Banjo had tried, Rupert began to unwind.

At the end of his account, Banjo expected a real telling off. Instead, Rupert slumped back in his chair in a state of relief and disbelief. Rupert said nothing. He just folded his arms around the back of his head and stared up at the ceiling. Rachel noticed a tear creep down Rupert's cheek. Then she spoke.

'He's special your Josh. No chance he'd have been hurt.'

'How do you mean, special?' said Rupert.

'Just accept it. He's being watched over, aren't you Josh lad?'

Josh had heard her say this before. *She must believe it.*

'He can stop here tonight in the spare room. Enough excitement for one day, eh?'

Rupert got up and gave Josh a long hug. At first, he didn't speak to Banjo but turned to him just before he left the room.

'Cheers.' Rupert glanced at Banjo. 'You did all right, mate.'

Banjo smiled and relaxed.

'Cool,' he replied.

*

When Mina called at Rachel's house the next morning she was dressed in her work costume. She startled Josh at first. It was the first time he had seen her up close. Mina saw the surprise in his face.

'Oh, sorry, Josh. Work clothes for later. I normally wear something more fancy.'

His eyes opened so wide he felt they would fall out. He was speechless. Rachel chuckled. Mina wore a long black and red dress with frills and black gloves that reached up to her elbows. Around her neck hung a spider shaped necklace and her hair was purple streaked with white. He gawped at her for some time but when she gave him a cuddle the initial shock drained away.

'Rupert says I've got to look after you so let's go have some fun. But maybe not as much as yesterday, eh?'

Although Josh was convinced that everybody would be staring at Mina in the streets, he was surprised that nobody paid them any attention. Occasionally they would pass someone else dressed similarly. At first, he couldn't help staring but gradually the strangeness wore off. *Maybe it's normal here.*

She took Josh on a tour of Whitby, finishing up at the spooky museum where he had seen Rupert talking to her. He looked at the sign above the door. 'The Dracula Experience'. At first, he wasn't sure he wanted to go inside because it looked fearsome with images of weird people in old costumes. Hesitating, he followed Mina into the building. She explained that it was a holiday attraction and it was her job to play the part of a ghost. Josh met the few people who worked there and although they appeared frightening at first in their unfamiliar clothes they were very friendly.

A man with red eyes and freaky hair introduced himself to Josh.

'Hi. I'm Frank. What do you think of all these? I hate them. Wouldn't think it with me working here would you?' he said, pointing at the imitations of bats flying around dark scenes of eerie buildings and graveyards.

Mina put her arm around Josh and showed him around, ending up in a small back room with a faded settee, a kitchen area and several items of old furniture. There were no windows so the only light was from a single bulb in the centre of the room. A sign on the door read Staff Room. Private.

Mina told Josh that, more than one hundred years ago, a man called Bram Stoker came to Whitby and wrote a book about an evil man called Count Dracula who arrived in the town by ship. She said it wasn't real so Josh needn't worry. 'The Dracula Experience' was just a bit of fun for holidaymakers. He asked if he could stay for a while so Mina pointed to some books on a shelf that he could read to pass the time. Then she made pretend ghost noises as she glided out of the door waving her arms.

'Just practising,' she said as she contorted her face then smiled. Josh giggled.

In the short time that Josh had been in Whitby he realised that not everything that appeared odd or creepy was dangerous. Often, they were just different. He was learning to test things out. Not to jump to conclusions or be scared when something or someone out of the ordinary emerged. Just be careful. Ask questions. Think.

Josh leafed through the books but nothing sparked his interest. He drifted around the room and drew back a curtain next to the kitchen area that concealed a small storage room. Bags, brushes, buckets. A discoloured book lay partly hidden on the floor. He picked it up, wiped the dust off it and was about to place it on the shelf with the other books when a page dropped out. The writing was strange and the words were arranged in a way that didn't make sense.

There was no visible page number so he flicked through the book to see if it fitted anywhere. When he compared the print in the book with the print on the single page they didn't match up. He wiped the book with the back of his hand and strained to read the washed out title. 'The Legend of Greycloak.' He folded the single page with care, placed it in his pocket and lay down on the settee to read.

Josh spent some of the day watching the actors as they appeared from dark corners making spooky noises to scare the visitors. Josh loved it when Frank, playing the part of Dracula, tried to frighten him when he wasn't looking but he couldn't stop himself laughing as the actor hovered over him menacingly.

'You're meant to be frightened, you know,' said Frank. 'I'll lose my job if I'm not scary.'

Josh apologised and, grinning, promised to be frightened the next time.

When Mina came to collect Josh at the end of the day he was still deep in his book.

'We're closing now. Josh? Josh?' She paused. 'There's a dalek and two cybermen behind you.'

Nothing.

She touched him lightly on the shoulder and said it was time to go.

'What are you reading?' she asked.

'There's this Viking warrior called Harald Greycloak. He was really bad to everyone in York and Whitby so the people got rid of him. Now Greycloak wants revenge.'

Mina said there was a story about an evil Viking stalking Whitby but there were so many tales around that nobody paid them much attention.

'Take it with you if you want,' she added. 'But remember it's just a story.'

'But why does it sound so real if it wasn't?'

Mina shrugged her shoulders but didn't reply. Even in the short time he had known her it seemed odd.

CHAPTER 7

Why does a friend become a best friend?

Mina and Josh walked back to Rupert's caravan but had to wait by the swing bridge to let a tall masted boat through from the harbour. Then up the old cobbled street to the one hundred and ninety nine steps leading to St Mary's Church. As they climbed, Josh noticed a fishy smell but this one was different.

'What's that smell?' asked Josh stopping to look at a thick, grey haze rising from a chimney nearby.

'Oh, it's Rupert's socks being cleaned.'

She nudged him and they both laughed.

'Not really. They're kippers,' said Mina. 'Herring soaked in salty water then cooked over a wood fire. Fancy one for tea?'

Mina bought three kippers and, as they started back up the steps, Josh bubbled over with what he had been reading, barely pausing for breath.

Half way up the steps he felt the breeze stir on his face, as if warning him. Looking up, he saw a pushchair with a toddler rolling down towards him followed by a distressed, screaming mother. Josh dropped his book, sprinted towards the pushchair and managed to grasp the bawling child before they toppled over the edge of the steps. Gasping, he wrapped his arms around the child until the mother arrived. She overflowed with gratitude and comforted the toddler as Mina caught up with them, clutching Josh's book.

'Hey, well done you,' said Mina. 'Extra rhubarb crumble for you tonight.'

As they approached the top of the steps, Josh felt a bite in the air and glimpsed a vague figure melting away in a haze through the churchyard. He stared at the fading image but was distracted when Mina ushered him away.

'Did you see that?' he asked her.

'You bet. You were a star. Come on, let's get tea and tell Rupert you're a hero.'

But that wasn't what Josh had meant. He looked back down the steps at the mother and child and wondered if there was a connection between the spectre and the near tragedy.

Josh spent the next two days reading 'The Legend of Greycloak' and trying to work out the writing on the loose page. But the page was full of old, swirly writing and it was hard to follow. A lot of the time he read in the abbey grounds with the breeze dancing round him. Josh couldn't get the image of the figure on the cliff top out of his head. *Why did Mina say 'it's just a story?'*

He thought about what Rachel had said. Why did she think he was so special? And who really was looking after him? A jumble of ideas scrambled through his mind and wouldn't go away. *I wish you were here mum.*

In the absence of his mum, Josh talked to the breeze. When the breeze blew, soft or strong, his friend would listen and speak in tones that seesawed with emotion. He imagined the breeze would carry his thoughts and words to his mum so he was always with her.

When Rover was around Josh would talk to him. Unless Rover was eating, in which case he would give Josh a funny look or walk away. When Josh spoke, Rover meowed back. If Rover closed his eyes to a question, Josh took that as a 'no'. But when the cat opened his eyes wide and stared, it felt like a 'yes.' The breeze and Rover comforted Josh whenever he felt alone.

*

Later in the week, Mina took Josh to a fair on the cliff top on the opposite side of the river from the abbey. It was only a small fair. Just a few rides and stalls dotted alongside the road that ran parallel with the beach below. The sweet smell of toffee apples and popcorn collided with the savoury aroma of onions and chips floating up from roadside kiosks. Josh looked on at the hurly burly of children buzzing from stall to stall and ride to ride. He grinned at two small boys eating candyfloss that stuck to their faces like balls of pink cotton wool. Music from a large organ accompanied the activity.

The carefree atmosphere emboldened Josh to ask Mina a question that had bounced around his head since he first saw her.

'Why do you wear funny clothes?'

Mina chuckled.

'Ever heard of Goths?'

Josh shook his head.

'It's a sort of fashion. Lots of people in Whitby dress like this. Cool isn't it?'

He nodded half-heartedly. Mina hugged him and kissed him on the cheek. Warmth radiated through him. Like when you feel loved.

Josh noticed a little girl crying. She was staring down at a melting blob of white, pink and green ice cream that had fallen from her cornet and was now sprawled on the path. Josh ran over and knelt down beside her. The little girl looked at him intently and stopped crying. Then she said something unintelligible as her mother arrived.

'Never mind, we'll get you another one.' She turned to Josh. 'Thank you for trying to help her. That was really kind. Would you like an ice cream?'

The little girl jumped up and down, the remains of her cornet still in her hand.

'Oh…thanks.' Josh turned to Mina who had been watching. She was talking with a friend who he now knew was also dressed in a Goth style with a purple dress and a black jacket.

'Is that okay?' asked Josh.

'Of course. I'm just popping over with Yasmine to haunt that shop. I'll spook you there in a minute.'

Mina glided away making ghostly noises. The lady and the little girl stared at Mina and her friend with fascination.

'Don't mind her, she's just a ghost,' said Josh. 'And a Goth.'

He thanked the lady for the ice cream and ate it hurriedly as the warmth of the sun made it trickle down over his fingers.

Crossing the road, Josh noticed two large black birds circling overhead. He recalled the birds he had seen in his garden at home and at Goathland. At that moment his friend, the breeze, swept over him and he turned to see a group of boys shouting at another boy who was carrying a huge, bright green toy frog. Josh stood and watched. Amidst the yelling, one of the group snatched the boy's toy from him and waved it above his head. The boy tried to grab it back. He began wrestling with them and even though he was outnumbered he didn't seem to care about his own safety. *There are too many of them.* Another of the group pushed the boy from behind and he tumbled to the ground as the others cheered.

As he got up, ready to take them on again, Josh dropped what remained of his ice cream and ran without thinking towards the group. He didn't know why but he shouted that there was a policeman coming. The group looked at Josh in astonishment and ran down a side street leaving the other boy alone, shouting after them.

'Are you all right?' asked Josh.

The boy said nothing but his face was strained with fury and he was about to run after the gang when Josh held his arm.

'Better not. There are more of them.'

'I don't care.'

He looked at Josh and began to calm down.

'They don't like me.'

'Why not?'

The boy brushed his clothes and examined a small tear in the knee of his trousers.

'Because I'm from another country.'

'So what,' said Josh. 'I'm not from here either. I'm from Leeds. My name's Josh.'

The boy rubbed his leg.

'Is it hurt?' asked Josh.

'It's all right, thanks. My name's Anders.'

Josh offered to walk home with Anders but first he ran to the shop to check with Mina. She agreed but said that Josh had to meet her at the café by six o'clock.

*

Ambling down the side streets, the boys stopped at a toyshop to examine the colourful display of cars, trains and animals. As they walked down the hill, they could see St Mary's church and the abbey through the gaps between the buildings. They appeared to be watching over them. At the bottom of the hill Josh noticed more churches; St John the Evangelist and St Hilda's with its white stone statues of two women looking up at Christ on the cross. *Why does Whitby have so many churches?*

Over the road by the swing bridge, they continued in the direction of the marina where seagulls glided, screeching above the masts of moored boats. They stopped outside a small restaurant with the name Kristjan's in blue and red letters on the window. Wooden tables and benches sat deserted outside the restaurant.

'It's my dad's restaurant,' said Anders pushing open the door to a large room that was empty apart from tables and chairs set for unknown customers. Paintings of an unfamiliar land of mountains and lakes hung on the walls.

'Pappa! It's me,' Anders called to the back of the restaurant.

A short, stocky man with a moustache wearing black trousers, a powder blue shirt and white apron emerged from the kitchen. He was wiping his hands on a towel.

'Good fair, Anders?' he asked in broken English.

'Some boys pushed me over and took a prize I won from a stall. This is Josh. He helped me.'

'My boy. You all right?'

'I'm fine pappa. But when I see them again I'm going to…'

'Okay, we talk later. You good boy, Josh. You hungry? I get krumkake.'

Anders' father ran out to the kitchen and returned with a plate full of freshly baked pastries.

'Eat, eat.'

'What are they?' asked Josh.

'Like rolled up cake,' said Anders. 'With cream and jam.'

Josh took one and sunk his teeth into the soft, sweet sponginess.

'Thank you, Josh. You good friend. My name Kristjan. From Norway. You welcome here any time.'

Josh bombarded them with numerous questions about Norway and how they came to England. Kristjan explained that his wife had died some years ago and he had decided to come with his only child, Anders, to seek a new life in England. Anders said he and his father used to live in a house overlooking the sea in a town called Bergen.

'The Viking warrior Harald Greycloak lived there,' said Anders.

As he said it, Kristjan touched Anders on his arm and shook his head.

'Pappa doesn't like me talking about it,' said Anders.

'I know about him,' said Josh. 'I've read 'The Legend of Greycloak".'

Anders looked at his father. Eventually Kristjan nodded in agreement.

'We could see the mountain called Ulriken from our house. It stood over our town, like it was protecting us somehow. Then, on midwinter's day, weird things started to happen. People having accidents and seeing a strange man.'

'What did the man look like?' asked Josh.

'You couldn't see him properly. There always seemed to be a mist around when he appeared. And these two big birds. Like really black.'

Kristjan shifted uneasily in his chair but Josh thought about the birds.

Anders continued.

'He used to watch us when we went out but he never did anything. Once, when we were driving back from town, he appeared in the middle of the road and we had to stop quickly. He just stood there pointing straight at us with a sword. Then as the mist rolled back he disappeared.'

Kristjan got up and started collecting the empty plates.

'It nothing,' said Kristjan.

'Why did he point at you?'

'I don't know,' replied Anders. 'But there was an old prophecy in our town about Greycloak having his revenge and people coming to stop him.'

'This just story,' said Kristjan but without conviction.

As they talked, Josh thought of telling them about the grey Viking warrior he had seen and the two large birds that appeared to follow him. Then a glance at the clock reminded Josh he had promised to meet Mina at six o'clock and the thought went out of his head.

'I've got go.' Josh turned to Anders. 'Do you want to go to the abbey tomorrow? It's great for exploring.'

Anders looked to his father.

'Okay.'

Josh thanked Kristjan for the krumkake and darted out of the restaurant. Anders called after him and when Josh glanced back the sight of his new friend made him stop. Anders was in the doorway making a sign of the cross and pointing towards him. Josh gave him a curious look then ran to see Mina.

*

As he approached Ruby's café, Josh's conversation with Anders and Kristjan bounced around in his head. Amidst the chaos he wished his mum was there. His heart burned at the thought of not being able to contact her because Rupert said she was too weak after her operation. The black cloud of going to Nathan's house loomed over him. Josh looked through the café window, like a giant television screen, at the people who were now his friends. He looked down at the ground and his eyes moistened. *Is this the last time?*

Anders

Mr & Mrs Symes

CHAPTER 8

Can people talk without speaking?

The night before Nathan was due to arrive, Josh sat in his room staring out of the window stroking Rover who was sprawled out on the chair next to his bed. The lighthouse appeared to flash more brightly than before and the wind chime tinkled more loudly as his friend glanced against the window, reminding him he was not alone. Josh didn't sleep. He lay awake wondering about Anders, Greycloak and the Bergen Prophecy and if he would ever return to Rupert's caravan. Rover stayed with him, sensing the change that was about to happen.

'You and me are mates aren't we?'

Rover purred and twitched his tail.

'Do you think I'll ever come back here?'

The cat opened his eyes wide, meowed and rested his paw on Josh's hand. He picked Rover up and held him close. For once, Rover let himself be held and didn't try to jump down.

The morning came too quickly for Josh. He delayed packing his case and watched the darkening clouds roll in. Rupert knocked on Josh's open bedroom door.

'You okay?'

Josh didn't reply but looked at Rupert with pleading eyes. He longed to stay but he had no choice. He understood he had only been allowed to stay a short time with Rupert but even so… If somebody was really looking after him, like Rachel had said, why did they give Josh all this happiness and new friends only to take them away again? *How could that be right?*

'I tried to convince your mum you should stay here, but…she still thought Nathan's would be best.'

Josh crumpled onto the bed and burst into tears for the first time in years. The emotions had built up and now overflowed. Rupert moved towards him and held him tight whilst Rover jumped up next to them meowing anxiously.

'Why can't I stay? It's not fair.'

'I really wish you could. I even said…'

'But I'm happy here,' implored Josh. 'Why can't I do what makes me happy?'

Rupert paused then said,

'Sometimes, buddy, we have to do things we don't want to. We may not realise, but it might be for the best.'

'Why is it for the best if it makes me unhappy?'

Rupert sighed. 'That's a toughie. There's always a reason for things even if we can't see it at first. Maybe it'll work out better than we hoped, eh?'

Rupert wasn't sure how it could work out better but he so wanted to make things right.

'Oh, nearly forgot. Rachel asked me to give you this,' said Rupert passing an envelope to Josh.

Josh opened the envelope and took out a note.

ALL THINGS WORK TOGETHER FOR GOOD TO THOSE WHO LOVE
From your loving Rachel

He studied it then looked inquisitively at Rupert who shrugged his shoulders. Josh folded the note and put it in his pocket.

'Oh, and Mina sends her love. She says she's always with you.'

Josh couldn't even force a smile.

*

Nathan arrived later that morning. He collected Josh's suitcase and took it to his car without saying anything.

'Josh can stay with me you know,' said Rupert.

Nathan waited for Josh who emerged on the front porch and hugged Rupert.

'Hang in there, buddy. We'll come and visit you.' Rupert didn't sound convincing.

Rover disappeared before Josh had a chance to say one last goodbye. As Nathan drove off, Josh turned round to wave. Rupert raised a weary hand back then stood still. Frozen.

A steady drizzle moistened the air and a sea fret had developed. Josh's thoughts were spinning. His mum, Anders, krumkake at Kristjan's, Ruby's café, Mina and her unusual clothes, Rachel's eyes, 'talking' Rover, bonkers Banjo and the human dustbin, Mountain. Now he was leaving them and going to Nathan's house where he should have been originally. Josh almost began wishing that Rupert hadn't collected him that day at Goathland. If he hadn't, Josh wouldn't now be so upset at leaving friends who had become so important to him. He would have been spared this heartache.

As Nathan turned left out of the caravan park, Josh noticed Rover trotting after them. He followed the car for a while then stopped as the car increased speed. The sea fret thickened.

Why didn't Anders come?

A short way down the road, Josh saw some people huddled together against the rain at the roadside. As the car approached them, one of the group stretched out an arm, hailing them to stop.

'Who on earth is that?' snapped Nathan. The car slowed down as it approached the group. Josh recognised them through the gloom.

'It's Mountain. And Rachel and Banjo.'

'Who?'

'Stop, uncle Nathan! Stop!'

Nathan pulled alongside the bedraggled party and Josh opened the window letting the rain sprinkle into the car.

'Easy,' said Banjo.

Mountain punched the air with one hand in his customary way. With the other hand he waved a fishing rod which he and Josh had often used together at the end of the pier. Then Rachel spoke.

'Get my note?'

'Yes. But what does it mean?'

'You'll see. Not long now, love. See you later.' Rachel winked but Josh was confused by her comments yet remarkably encouraged. *Later?*

'Put that window up! The seats are getting wet,' protested Nathan.

Josh wanted to ask if they had seen Anders but Nathan drove off leaving the three friends in the rain. Josh looked back at them through the rear window and re-read the note Rachel had given him.

ALL THINGS WORK TOGETHER FOR GOOD TO THOSE WHO LOVE

Nathan drove away from town and from everyone and everything Josh had come to love. When they slowed down at a crossroads, Josh saw a boy standing on an embankment with his bike. In spite of the rain he wasn't wearing a jacket. *He must be freezing.*

'Anders!'

Josh was puzzled at how Anders knew he would be coming that way but his spirit rose and he waved vigorously. He caught a glimpse of Anders smiling and wanted to ask Nathan to stop but he accelerated, driving Josh towards an uncertain future.

*

It took twenty minutes to drive to Nathan's house through the smothering dampness. The car turned off the road through a pair of tall, black iron gates and along a driveway that twisted through wooded grounds. An old man was picking up petals from a flowerbed and putting them into a round, green bin. He stared at Josh but showed no emotion as the car passed by.

The sand coloured Yorkshire stone house, built on three levels, looked like two houses joined together, each with its own sloping roof. On the left and right ends of the house were two tall chimneys. Nathan stopped the car in front of a great wooden front door with a brass knocker in the shape of a cross. He thought he'd seen it somewhere before.

'Is this your house?' asked Josh.

'That's what comes from working hard,' replied Nathan. 'Don't just sit there gawping. Get your suitcase.'

Nathan got out and ran towards the front door out of the wet. Josh sat in the car looking back at the old man who was still staring at him.

Josh struggled in the fine rain to get the suitcase out of the car boot. It was too heavy to lift as well as carrying his rucksack so he dragged it across the wet ground. He all but fell through the doorway into the house.

'Don't scratch the floor!' shouted Nathan from half way up a spiral staircase in front of Josh. An old lady appeared from a side door and trudged towards the bedraggled guest.

'You're drenched, boy. I'll fetch a towel. Can't have you dripping everywhere.'

She disappeared as quickly as she had arrived but Nathan continued up the staircase and out of view. For a few minutes, Josh stood alone in his damp clothes gazing around him at the size of the house. A soft grey light shone through the tall church-like windows into the vast, timber-panelled hall. He noticed that several panels had lines carved into them at various angles almost like letters but without any curves. Through an open door to the right he saw what looked like a library with rows of drearily covered books stacked from floor to ceiling. The house smelled of polish and inhospitality. Everything was dark. No colour. He thought he heard someone talking to him in a muffled voice but when Josh looked around he was alone in the hall. He shivered.

The old lady reappeared through a different door from the one by which she left. It surprised Josh and made him curious as to where the doors led. The pendulum of a tall, narrow clock at the end of the hall swayed backwards and forwards wearily.

'Here, dry yourself off. Follow me.'

The old lady helped Josh with his suitcase up the same spiral staircase where Nathan had gone earlier.

'In here,' motioned the old lady to Josh. 'I'm Mrs Symes.'

'Who's the man in the garden?'

'Mr Symes. Lunch is in the dining room at one o'clock. Mr Nathan doesn't like people being late. Put your wet clothes outside your door. I'll wash them later.'

She left Josh in a large room with a dark brown wardrobe, one lonely chair, a chest of drawers and an old wrought iron bed. The bed was bigger than he was used to and was covered with a washed out pea green bedspread designed with various old fashioned sailing ships. A drab picture of Whitby abbey hung by the door; a reminder of the happiness he had left behind. Although twice the size of his bedroom at home, this one was less welcoming. The ceilings were high and every sound Josh made echoed around the room that had no carpet. Only rough wood floors. Even though there was no Rover to talk to, Josh felt there was a presence in the house, which seemed like it was trying to speak to him.

Josh put on some dry clothes and left the damp ones outside his bedroom door as Mrs Symes had instructed. He didn't unpack immediately, hoping somehow that if he kept his things in the suitcase then maybe his mum would telephone Nathan and say Josh could go back to Rupert's. It was a bleak hope but one he clung to for several days. The only items he took out were 'The Legend of Greycloak', his cherished photograph, which he put on the window sill so the light would brighten it, and the wind chime to alert him of his friend's presence. He hung the wind chime on a curtain tieback by the window.

As he positioned the photograph, Josh glanced out at the garden. The old man, who he now knew as Mr Symes, was peering up at Josh's window. *Why is he staring at me?* Although unsettled by the old man's behaviour, Josh felt he should try and talk to him. But he didn't know why. At one time, Josh would have been frightened to approach the old man but his experiences in Whitby had given him more confidence. Nonetheless, he knew that he still had to be careful and decided to wait until Mrs Symes was around. The rain persisted.

Josh heard the clock in the hall wake up and strike one o'clock. He remembered Mrs Symes's words about being late. He bolted out of his room and down the stairs but stopped in the hall. *Which one's the dining room?* Nathan appeared at one of the doors leading off the hall.

'Not a good start is it? Didn't Mrs Symes say one o'clock?'

'Yes. Sorry.'

Like everything else in the house, the dining room was old. The same dismal panelling on the walls except, on one side, for three large rectangular windows made up of six panels in each. Some of the panels had coloured glass shapes that provided the only colour in a sombre room. The windows looked out onto the front lawn. Josh sat down at the end of the table nearest the windows and looked out at the driveway leading to the main road and Whitby beyond.

Mrs Symes gave Nathan and Josh their lunch. Fish with the head and skin left on, which took Josh aback when he first saw it, and a selection of vegetables. Even though the food looked wonderful Josh had no appetite. His stomach felt like a great bag of sand and his heart was split between his mum and Whitby. He knew his mum wanted him to be with Nathan but he still didn't understand why. Josh started to ask Mrs Symes a question as she poured a white sauce next to his fish but she placed a finger over her lips. Nathan looked up from his plate.

'That's one of my principal rules. No talking at the table.'

Josh forced himself to eat the fish, picking away the skin and the head to reveal pink flesh. The rest of the meal took place in silence except for the clanking of cutlery on crockery. Although Josh was grateful for the food, he would have gladly traded it for doughnuts at Ruby's café or meat stew at Kristjan's. He thought how more enjoyable meal times were when they were shared with chattering, laughing friends.

When they had finished their meal, Nathan turned to Josh.

'As you know, I have rules in this house. If you're not sure of them Mrs Symes will tell you. You'll have to entertain yourself. I'm far too busy to spend time with you. My room, the study and the basement are strictly out of bounds.'

'Have you got any pets?' asked Josh.

'Definitely not! They're a nuisance and I've told Mr Symes to get rid of any rabbits or squirrels he finds in the grounds.'

Nathan said he would see Josh at seven o'clock sharp for tea.

If Josh got hungry before then he should see Mrs Symes in the kitchen. Nathan left him alone in the dining room looking out of the window. The rain had stopped and Mr Symes had gone.

Josh expected to see birds outside but saw nothing. The only movement was from his friend, the breeze, rustling the trees, urging him to come outside and revel in the warm dampness.

'You'll never leave me will you?' he whispered.

'Talking to yourself?' said Mrs Symes reappearing to clear the table.

'Oh…no…just…where's Mr Symes?'

'Taking lunch in the kitchen.'

'Can I meet him?'

'What you want to do that for?'

He looked away. Mrs Symes shook her head and tutted. Josh thought for a while then continued.

'I want to tell him a story.'

'Mr Symes doesn't care for stories.'

'Perhaps he hasn't heard any good ones yet.'

'We have got a shrewd one haven't we? I'll ask him. Wait here while I take the dishes through.'

As Josh waited, he was drawn to a portrait of a lady with flowing hair that was hanging at the other end of the dining room. Dressed in white with a cloak of feathers, she was holding a shield in one arm and on the other arm, a bird whose feathers were a mosaic of white and steel. Josh was captivated. The lady was beautiful. Images of Rachel and the lady on the cliff top flashed in front of him then evaporated.

'Looks like you've caught him on a good day,' said Mrs Symes returning from the kitchen.

'Who's the lady in the painting?'

'You don't want to concern yourself with that. Come on if you want to tell that story of yours.'

Mrs Symes led Josh into the kitchen where her husband was eating baked beans on toast. The old man stopped with his fork half way to his mouth and got up from his chair when Josh appeared.

'I'm Josh,' he said holding out his hand. Mr Symes shook Josh's hand and held it for some while. The two appeared frozen in time as they looked at each other curiously. Mrs Symes watched them with hands on hips.

'You two got stuck?'

The look on Mr Symes's face suggested that he recognised Josh even though they had never met before.

'Let's have this story then,' said Mrs Symes, her impatience increasing as she busied herself with the washing up.

Josh explained about his mum's illness, that he expected to come to Nathan's house earlier but his uncle Rupert had met him at Goathland. He talked about the episode with Banjo and how he felt safe because Rachel said that he was special and she'd been looking forward to seeing him even though he didn't know anything about her. Mr Symes dropped his fork on the floor.

'What's with you? Seen a ghost?' said Mrs Symes retrieving the fork.

Mr Symes grabbed his hat and jacket and left the kitchen through the side door leading to the garden.

'What about your…? Oh, that man! His mind's always somewhere else. Never been the same since old Mr Haxby died. Pay no attention to him, he goes a bit yonderly. And let's get one thing straight; I'll have no fanciful ideas. I get enough of them with Mr Symes. Be off with you now!'

*

Josh slipped away to the garden to find Mr Symes and ask him why he reacted oddly to what Rachel had said. He wandered round to the back of the house and found a small brick building, the size of a large shed. He looked inside. It was the earthy smell that hit Josh first. He couldn't see the old man amongst the garden forks, spades and sacks of manure that were scattered randomly on the floor and the shelves that were piled high with all sizes of pots and cans. He called out for Mr Symes then a banging and clattering resounded from behind a shelf full of paint tins.

Someone moved from behind the shelf. Josh was shaken at first but recovered when he realised it was Mr Symes.

'Why did you leave when I said that about Rachel?'

The old man stood in the half-light. Unmoving. Staring. Silent. Then he gave Josh a number of plastic sacks and a pair of gloves and motioned to him to follow. Josh spent the rest of the afternoon clearing dead leaves, twigs and flowers from the grounds. Occasionally his friend would tease Josh by whipping up the leaves he had stacked up. Josh laughed at the game being played and joined in, romping around the garden. Mr Symes observed Josh for several minutes although his young helper was caught up in the moment and didn't notice.

Whenever Josh asked a question Mr Symes just nodded, said 'Aye' or 'Nay' and busied himself with work. Josh wanted to know more about the house. How come Nathan lived there? Who was old Mr Haxby? And who was the lady in the painting? He wondered if Mr Symes was holding something back.

A cheeky squirrel decided to venture into the gardens. In spite of what Nathan had told him, Josh talked to it and fed it an apple that had fallen from the giant tree next to the front gate. The old man watched him closely but he was distracted when the squirrel raced off and Josh stared down the driveway towards the gate. Mr Symes looked back and forth between Josh and…what?

Josh saw a whirling mist. A grey Viking warrior emerged from the gloom. The warrior took a few steps up the driveway but stopped for no reason. The warrior appeared unable to move forward but Josh could not see anything blocking his way.

Retreating back into the mist the warrior disappeared. Josh breathed more freely and turned to Mr Symes who gave him a bewildered but sympathetic look. *Does he know something?*

CHAPTER 9

Where does a key fit when every door already has one?

Josh ensured he was in the dining room for seven o'clock as he didn't want to annoy his uncle again but Nathan hadn't yet appeared. He sat down at the same seat as before and watched the clock crawl to seven o'clock. Josh wondered if anyone had tried to contact him but couldn't get through.

Then that same voice he heard before. Vague. Echoing. Yet near. *Maybe outside?* Josh got up and looked out of the window. No one.

'Who's there?'

An icy hollow rose up in his stomach.

Josh was about to go into the kitchen when Mrs Symes arrived and said that Nathan had to go out urgently on business so Josh would have to eat alone. He asked if he could eat in the kitchen with Mr and Mrs Symes since the idea of eating alone in such a large room wasn't appealing.

'The very idea,' said Mrs Symes. 'Mr Nathan wouldn't approve.'

Josh kept asking until, eventually, she gave in, but only on the condition that he would go back to the dining room if Nathan returned. Josh agreed and followed Mrs Symes to the kitchen, glancing again at the portrait of the lady whose eyes seemed to follow him as he left. Josh sensed that she was speaking to him. *Was that her voice?* He hesitated then hurried after Mrs Symes.

He sat at the table listening to Mrs Symes muttering about children being in the house but Mr Symes ate in silence, looking up only occasionally to glance at Josh.

'Who's that lady in the painting? The one in the dining room?' Josh asked Mr Symes, hoping he would have more chance of getting an answer. He was about to reply but Mrs Symes interrupted.

'Never come in the rest of the house do you?'

Mr Symes shook his head.

'Why not?' asked Josh.

The old man stopped eating and looked intently at his wife. Again she replied for her husband.

'He won't. Out of some daft loyalty isn't it? Worse than a dog he is.'

'What loyalty?'

'It's no concern of yours,' Mrs Symes added, taking out an egg and ham salad in a frosted glass bowl from the fridge.

Josh suspected that Mr Symes wanted to say something even though his wife didn't want him to. He knew Nathan wouldn't tell him anything, but if he could get Mr Symes to talk more openly then he might start to learn more about the house. Especially the painting. And that voice.

Josh played with his salad, looked out of the window and longed for the time when his mum would soon be well so he could return home from his exile.

After tea, Josh spent the evening exploring the library looking for clues about the house and the lady in the painting. He spotted more carvings in wood panels and doors, similar to those in the hall. Running his fingers over the inscriptions, he hoped they would reveal their secrets but they remained silent.

Josh went to bed discouraged yet determined to find out more about the house. He looked in his rucksack and suitcase for his mobile phone hoping to text Anders but discovered he had left it at Rupert's. Lying in bed with the curtains open, Josh watched the moon casting a shadowy glare on the photo of him and his mum.

'All things work together for good to those who love,' he whispered as he started to re-read 'The Legend of Greycloak'.

*

The monotonous routine of meals and helping an indifferent Mr Symes continued for several days until Nathan announced one morning that he would be away on business overnight and would not be returning until the next day.

Nathan left after breakfast so Josh seized the chance to explore the library for clues. The main thing that struck him was that there appeared to be a large number of very old books about Viking mythology. Flicking through them, he discovered that marks like the woodcarvings around the house were called runes and they were Viking letters. Yet their real meaning was still a mystery. After a morning of checking as many books as he could, he resolved to break one of Nathan's rules.

The study was further down the hall with the key still in the lock. Josh looked around him before turning the key and easing the door open. Inside, it was brighter than the other rooms Josh had seen so far. Various sized, brown-tinged photographs of people in old style clothes by a harbour decorated the walls. A large fireplace dominated one end. At right angles to this was a large square window with a seat looking out on to the garden. Except for a wooden desk with a roll up front at the other end of the room, the only other contents were three leather chairs lined up against the wall and a rocking chair nestled in one corner.

A broad shaft of light streamed in through the window highlighting particles of dust that danced in the still air. An ornate silver clock on the desk beat out a tired rhythm. The warmth and brightness of the study provided a welcome retreat from the dimness of the rest of the house. Yet there was little to encourage Josh to stay long. No books to investigate and the photographs offered no pointers in his search for information about the house.

He was about to leave when he saw that the desk roller front was slightly open. He pulled it up carefully making sure that he disturbed none of the contents. Inside the desk were several pens, a stack of brown envelopes, some writing paper and an internal drawer that was locked. He looked for the key and found it in a small tray at the back of the desk. He tried to unlock the drawer but it didn't budge at first. Only when he experimented by turning the key backwards and forwards twice each way did he discover that the lock only worked in a sequence of turns. When he did manage to open it he found an untitled book bound in scratched black leather. Josh took it out and sat in the rocking chair. He wanted to sit in the window seat where the sun flooded in but he chose to stay out of sight in the corner.

On the first page, in faint lettering, he could just make out a heading 'The Bergen Prophecy.' A chill bit through him and he almost dropped the book as he recalled the words Anders had told him. The style of writing was the same as the loose page that had fallen from 'The Legend of Greycloak.' He couldn't read all of the contents properly because the ink had faded and the writing was unusual. The words made no sense and, in any case, were marked with damp patches.

As he skimmed through it, a small picture, the size of a postcard, fell out onto the floor. Josh picked it up. Immediately he recognised it as the same picture in the dining room, but smaller and in not so many colours. On the back he read the words, 'Freyja, Shield Maiden of the Houses of the White Settlement.' He returned the book and the picture to the desk then ran into the dining room to check the pictures were the same. Excitement fizzed through him when he realised they matched.

Returning to lock the study door, he then ran back to the kitchen where Mrs Symes was baking bread.

'Who's Freyja and what's a Shield Maiden?' exclaimed Josh.

'Mr Nathan's not one for talk and you'd best remember that.'

Josh studied her as she mixed flour, water, butter and a little salt in a round yellow bowl. Josh dipped his fingers in some flour which had spilled on the table and watched her knead everything together with her bare hands until it became a soft, spongy ball. The smell took him back to another time. He saw his mum before she was ill. Singing. Laughing as she daubed flour on Josh's nose whilst he nibbled on the unbaked pastry. A lump welled up in Josh's throat and his chest became heavy.

The clatter of a metal spoon on the tiled floor catapulted Josh back to the present. Mrs Symes picked it up and started to roll out the dough on the table top, ignoring Josh. He chewed on some leftovers and walked aimlessly around the kitchen. His mind kept churning up questions as the aroma of fresh, warm baking drifted around.

'Why won't Mr Symes talk to me?'

'Don't mind him. He's harmless as they come.'

Josh slumped down into a chair and fiddled with a wooden pastry brush that he spun round on the honey coloured wooden kitchen table. Mrs Symes glanced at him and shook her head.

'So why doesn't Mr Symes come into the house and…?'

'Whoa, lad!'

She stopped pressing out the dough, put her hands on her hips and sighed deeply.

'You don't give up do you?'

Wiping her hands on her apron, she took a recently poured cup of tea from the worktop and sat down at the table with Josh.

'He's loyal to old Mr Robert Haxby who lived here before Mr Nathan. Mr Robert built this house.'

Checking behind her at the kitchen door, she peeked out of the window and leaned towards Josh before speaking in a low tone.

'Mr Symes thinks this house....'

She stopped in mid sentence, leaned back then raised her voice a level.

'Anyway, he says he'll never step foot inside the house proper 'til the rightful owner returns. He only comes in the kitchen because he has to eat. Don't you be getting no notions and don't pay too much attention to him. He gets muddled. Fairy tale stuff most of it. Doesn't pay to be getting too nosey. Might find something you shouldn't. I've said too much already and, besides, you ought not to be here.'

'But those carvings on…?'

At that moment Mr Symes appeared at the back door.

'Enough talk now,' she said turning towards the old man. 'And have you fettled that squeaky front gate?' Mr Symes walked straight back out.

*

When he thought that Mrs Symes was preoccupied with the baking, Josh sneaked back to the study. He glimpsed something he'd missed earlier. Behind the door, neatly arranged on a small table, were six Babushka dolls, each one painted with a wide-eyed cat. They reminded him of Rover. He rearranged the dolls so they were not in height order but as he did, he noticed that one of the painted cats was winking. For an instant, he saw Rachel winking at him and he smiled to himself. Continuing to reorganise the dolls, he knocked one of them off the table. It was the doll with the winking cat. The doll split in half and Josh saw that something had fallen from it. He crawled around the carpet until he found the object. A key. Shining and smooth. As if it had rarely been used.

Josh put the doll together, placed it back on the table and examined the key, curious as to what it might open. Looking around the study, he couldn't see anything that seemed large enough. He tried the roller shutter on the desk but the key was much too big. It looked more like a door key but the study door already had one. Josh considered asking Mrs Symes but decided against it, thinking it would only get him into trouble.

He paced around the study rolling the key around in his hands, puzzling over what to do next. His thoughts bounced backwards and forwards between putting the key back and trying to work out where it fitted. *Why was the key in a doll?* Josh looked again at the winking cat. His friend rattled the window and he knew what he wanted to do. He returned to the kitchen but there was no trace of Mrs Symes. Just the comforting warmth of baking. Josh called out for her and checked some other rooms. Nothing.

As he stood in the hallway clutching the key in both hands, the anonymous voice briefly resurfaced in a low murmur. Josh's heart beat faster. Then the voice disappeared yet somehow it inspired him. He returned to the kitchen and poured a glass of tap water that he gulped. Trembling. Stomach knotting.

Josh tried all the doors on the ground floor but the key fitted none of them. He ran up the stairs, stumbling at the top in his impatience to try all the other possibilities. Glancing down the stairs, Josh checked to see that Mrs Symes had not reappeared but there was no movement. Only the sleepy strokes of the hall clock.

The last door was Nathan's room. Josh walked hesitantly down the corridor. He stared at the lock for some while, his courage draining from him like a bath emptying. He crept back towards the stairs but as he got there, curiosity ballooned inside him driving him back to the door. Without thinking, he slotted the key directly into the lock and... nothing. The lock didn't budge. There was no explanation. He'd tried every other lock he could find.

There must be somewhere else. Josh strained to recall where Nathan had said he shouldn't go. My room...the study...and... and...the basement.

'Basement!!'

Unthinking, Josh blurted it out and ran down the stairs. But he didn't know how to get to the basement. Every key must have a door. *Where's the door?*

The kitchen maybe? He had already tried the kitchen doors but the key didn't fit any of them. Although wary of being seen by Mr Symes, Josh went outside to the garden to check other options. He drew a blank. When Josh came back in, his friend wafted through and blew aside a curtain that had previously concealed a door. Josh smiled to himself. He looked back outside to check Mr Symes was not coming back in then ran into the hall to ensure there was no sign of Nathan or Mrs Symes. When he returned to the kitchen, Josh took two deep breaths, slid the key into the lock with a shaky hand and closed his eyes.

The lock turned. Josh eased the door open. Blackness. And the beginning of a staircase leading downwards. Groping around at the top of the stairs, he found a light switch and turned it on. The stairs were now dimly lit and although a damp, musty smell came up from below, Josh felt the need to check out the reason why Nathan had banished him from this part of the house.

Yet after only two steps his nerve cracked like a dry twig and he darted back into the kitchen, hurling himself onto a chair. He gazed at the staircase and waited until his heart slowed down. Josh stayed there for several minutes until the chiming hall clock startled him. Looking through the windows, he saw tree branches swaying and knew he had no reason to be afraid. Josh got up and inched his way towards an uncertain descent.

With caution, he made his way down the steps gripping the key and shutting the door behind him. Josh felt the rough coolness of the walls as he steadied himself in the half-light. A stale smell drifted up to meet him. The basement was small, uncluttered and only covered the area below the kitchen. He had imagined something larger. Two grey metal filing cabinets hugged the back wall and a number of old paintings were stacked on their sides on the floor at the foot of the stairs. A swivel chair with a dull brown seat and frayed backrest sat alongside the paintings. An unshaded light bulb hung above a square, grey marble-top table in the centre of the room. Josh was puzzled why Nathan didn't want him to go down there. *Nothing here.*

Josh looked back up the stairs. Quiet. He opened the filing cabinets in turn but found only mouldy newspapers and magazines. The headline on a copy of one newspaper read:

NEW OWNER FOR MYSTERY HOUSE

He scanned the first few words of the article but nothing interested him so Josh put it back in the drawer. His early excitement had now evaporated and he sighed. *Is that all?* Turning back up the steps he spotted a square metal box partly obscured by the stack of paintings. He knelt down on the smooth tiled floor and slipped the box out. It was locked and didn't respond to the key Josh had used for the basement door. He checked the filing cabinets to see if they contained any keys but found nothing.

When he turned round he tripped over a loose floor tile. Josh looked back up the stairs to confirm he was still alone. Hush.

Stooping down, he lifted up the tile revealing a clear plastic bag holding a key. He removed the key from the bag and tried it in the metal box. It opened without a problem.

Inside the metal box was a beige coloured envelope secured with a dark red ribbon. Josh sat on the bottom step and put the envelope on his knees before untying the ribbon. He pulled out a number of folded papers, some of which were hand written and some printed. One of them was headed up 'Will' in a large decorative style and he saw the name Robert Haxby. The rest was difficult to read because it had faded although he could make out some words. He gasped as he saw more names further down the page. Nathan Haxby. Then Rupert Haxby and Lucy Haxby which had lines drawn through them.

'Mum!' Josh called out.

Realising what he'd done, he looked up to the top of the stairs fearing somebody might have heard him. Josh held his breath expecting to hear Mrs Symes call out. But there was only silence and he started breathing again. He read on, still unsure about what a 'will' meant and why his mum's name was on it. Or Nathan's and Rupert's come to that. Josh flicked through the rest of the papers, including a typed letter from Robert Haxby to Runswick Solicitors, but he didn't understand that either.

Another set of papers fascinated Josh more. The name Robert Haxby was handwritten many times on several sheets of paper. It reminded him of how he had to practice handwriting when he was at primary school. *Why would anyone do that if they didn't have to?* Josh got up and swung on the chair baffled as to what the papers were about.

He was returning them to the envelope when he heard a sound at the top of the steps. Josh froze. Hearing nothing more, he put the ribbon in the box, which he placed behind the paintings. He kept the papers. Dropping the key into the bag, he tossed it into the gap in the floor and reset the tile on top. Josh edged towards the foot of the steps.

Looking up, he saw that the door was open. The silhouette of a man loomed at the top. Josh had nowhere to hide and the only way out was blocked by the strange figure. Beads of sweat bloomed on Josh's brow and his hands became clammy. Breath shallow. Throat dry.

Terror overwhelmed Josh making his legs weak and his heart thud. Silence the only sound. Everything stood still. Nobody moved. Stop.

Then, inexplicably, the figure moved away from the top of the steps without saying a word, leaving the light on and the door open. Josh waited several minutes before moving again.

When the figure didn't reappear and there was no further sound, Josh slunk back up the steps gripping the envelope of papers close to his chest. Something brushed past his ear that startled him. Spinning around, he saw that a cobweb had fallen from the ceiling and clung to the side of the wall with a spider dangling from it.

He continued up the steps, switched off the light and peeked around the door before shutting and locking it. Then he ran back to the study, put the key back in the Babushka doll and scampered back to his room. Once inside, he slammed the door shut and ducked behind his bed. Gasping for air, he looked around for some assurance amongst the turmoil. The photograph of him and his mum and the gentle music of his friend swishing at the window calmed him.

Josh re-examined the papers to see whether he could make any more sense of them but most were unintelligible until he found one particular letter. A red seal first drew his attention. Signed by Robert Haxby it read:

I, ROBERT HAXBY, BEING OF SOUND MIND AND BODY, DO HEREBY AMEND MY WILL AS FOLLOWS. ALL MY ESTATE SHALL, UPON MY DEATH, BE GIVEN TO MY SON, NATHAN HAXBY. THE ESTATE TO INCLUDE MY HOUSE, MONEY AND ALL OTHER PERSONAL BELONGINGS.

Signed,

Robert Haxby

The signature on the letter was the same as the practise writing. *What's that about? Must tell someone.* He knew he didn't want to tell Nathan. Mr Symes? He wondered about it but didn't think he knew him well enough. Pushing the papers under his mattress, Josh went over to the windowsill and clutched the photograph close to his chest before curling up on the bed. Everyone was out of reach.

Except the voice. Still there. Tender.

CHAPTER 10

Can a picture tell a story?

Josh had tea by himself that night. Not in the kitchen with Mrs Symes but in the cavernous dining room. He suspected that Nathan had found out and had told her off. Picking at his tuna fish bake and broccoli, Josh stared at the portrait of Freyja the Shield Maiden. She appeared to be staring straight back at him, smiling, trying to tell him something. He shuddered at the idea of a painting talking to him. Yet why did the lady have such a calming influence on him and why did he keep seeing Rachel? *That's silly.* He couldn't get the thought out of his head. Josh wondered if the voice he kept hearing was hers but he rejected the idea because it sounded deeper. More like a man.

Mr Symes occasionally passed by the window tending the garden and casting casual glances inside. Josh's stomach tensed and relaxed as his thoughts seesawed. He fidgeted in his chair, taking an odd bite of food in between daydreams.

'Not sick are you?' asked Mrs Symes, reappearing without warning. 'Can't be doing with you sick.'

'Oh, no. I'm fine thank you.'

She muttered under her breath as she flitted around the room dusting and looking at Josh. He thought of Anders in Whitby. How many bacon sandwiches had Mountain eaten that day and was Banjo still as dippy? Were Rachel and Mina still thinking about him and had Rupert managed to convince his mum to let Josh go back to the caravan? Tears stung his eyes.

Unseen by Mrs Symes, the Shield Maiden held out her arms

beckoning Josh. He got up, walked towards her and listened to her honey voice tell him about astonishing tales of a prophecy fulfilled, the grey man and winter marching across the sea. She revealed extraordinary visions that spun around him as in a dream. Yet Josh wasn't asleep. Nor did he feel completely awake. It was half-wake. Trying to make order from the tangle of images, he thought he heard her say 'Search the kennings' but before he could ask her what they were, Mrs Symes accidentally knocked a silver candle holder from the sideboard onto the floor and startled him back to now.

'I think I'll go up to my room. Can I finish this later?'

Mrs Symes tutted, removed Josh's plate and left. Josh was leaving when Mr Symes appeared by the window. For the first time, he smiled. Only a vague smile but it was the most feeling he had ever shown. Josh was so surprised that he walked into a chair. Mr Symes lingered for a moment then walked across the lawn collecting fallen leaves in a green, garden waste sack. Josh toyed with the cords on his hooded top and went back up to his room. He lay down on the bed and allowed himself to cry. He thought about his mum and talked to her with his eyes closed whilst his friend carried his words off to her. Josh relaxed then fell asleep.

When he woke up, it was almost dark outside. He sat up and wished he had his mobile phone but that wasn't an option. Josh re-read Rachel's note for what seemed like the one hundredth time.

ALL THINGS WORK TOGETHER FOR GOOD TO THOSE WHO LOVE

He put the note back in his pocket and sat still for a while, watching the blankness outside. Although he still did not understand what Rachel meant, he recalled her words that someone was looking after him. From deep inside, Josh felt a rising strength to do something.

'What should I do, mum?'

He shut his eyes and saw her smiling. Thoughts cascaded through Josh's mind but he couldn't put them into any order. Then he saw Rachel sitting in the café with Rover. She winked at him and one idea screamed out above the others. *Go. Go now. Go to Whitby. Tell people about it.* Josh scrambled off his bed and looked out across the grounds that swayed with the shadows of trees and bushes. Doubts rose up to oppose his newfound confidence. He didn't know the way to Whitby, especially at night. *What if I get lost?*

Then another wave of courage flooded through his body compelling him to leave. Josh paced around his room, checked the documents he had pushed under his mattress and looked at the photo of him and his mum. He opened his window slightly and a cool, fresh smell rolled in with his friend who tinkled a greeting with the wind chime.

By the time night had taken a full grip Josh was determined to leave. Mr and Mrs Symes were asleep and Nathan was still away. Josh knew where he could find a torch. By the time anybody woke up, he would be back in Whitby with everyone. Safe. *Won't I?*

He took the documents, his most treasured possessions and a few clothes and put them in his rucksack. His suitcase was far too heavy to take with him so he decided to leave it behind with the rest of his belongings.

Josh sat on his bed, ready to go but still searching for final approval from somewhere that he was doing the right thing. His courage started to melt. Then his friend rapped the window again giving him the push he needed.

He slipped open the bedroom door and edged his way down the stairs. Night noises broke the still of the house. Wood creaking. Clock ticking. A fox howled eerily outside. Tree shadows skipped on the walls, tempting him to return to the safety of his room but Josh drove himself though the invisible curtain of fear. Then the voice. Softer but more distinct. He thought he caught the words 'come back' but he dismissed it, blaming the night.

At the bottom of the stairs he turned past the library and took the front door key from its hook in the hallway. Before he could grasp it, the kitchen door opened. An outline of a figure stood in the murkiness. Josh gasped and stumbled backwards against the wall. He clenched his fists together. Heart racing. Body stiffening. Mouth open. Josh pressed himself harder against the wall as the figure approached. Then it stopped a metre or so away from him, still in shadow.

A cloud drifted away, exposing the moonlight that shone through the landing window onto the thin, craggy features of a man.

'Me. Symes,' said the figure.

Josh didn't know what to feel. The old man's behaviour had never been predictable.

'Been watching. Follow me.'

Barely able to speak, Josh forced out some garbled words.

'Why should I go with you?'

'Can help. Found something didn't you? In the basement?'

Josh's head was reeling, his thoughts rebounding between staying and going. Mrs Symes's words about her husband never entering the rest of the house escaped Josh amidst all the rumpus.

Mr Symes continued. 'Get you back to Whitby. Tell people.'

The urge to get back to Whitby swept through Josh who peeled himself away from the wall, clutching his rucksack, fearing the old man might wrench it from him. Signalling to Josh to follow, Mr Symes took the key then eased the door shut and locked it behind them. Warily, Josh followed him a few steps behind.

'Know the way. Stay close,' whispered the old man.

They stole down the driveway, the gravel crunching underfoot. High trees swayed above them on both sides cutting out what light there was. Josh felt his way along the low stone wall towards the front gate but Mr Symes appeared to need no assistance. It was as if some invisible force was guiding him in the right direction. Josh glanced back to the house and sensed that he was leaving something, or someone, behind. *What is it?*

Approaching the road, a streetlight smouldered through the darkness and Josh picked out the shapes of houses. Beyond the houses the light dimmed and the night spread its dark cloak over the countryside. Mr Symes turned on his torch and Josh followed his silhouette along the narrow country lane. There was no pavement so the old man led the way keeping to the side, occasionally turning around to ensure Josh was still following.

Up ahead, Josh noticed a pale white creature shuffling high amongst the shadowy branches of an oak tree. Then the ghostly shape stopped moving as they came near. Josh scurried alongside Mr Symes and, as they walked beneath it, the creature turned to follow their movements. A shiver like an electric charge shot through Josh but it was cut short when he heard a familiar sound. A hoot, a disturbance in the branches and the barn owl flew off into the night to continue its hunting. Relieved, Josh let out an audible breath.

'All right?'

'Mm,' Josh replied.

Josh wasn't sure he was all right but he wanted to be. Josh was living by faith.

Tightness gripped Josh's body as he tried to keep pace with his long-striding guide. Yet in spite of all the uncertainty and strangeness of the situation, he was grateful the old man was there. Josh considered the people who had helped him recently. Before his arrival in Whitby, if he had seen the likes of Banjo or Mountain, he would have made every effort to avoid them. But now he realised that it wasn't always the most well dressed, normal looking people who were the kindest. Help sometimes came from those he least expected.

Trudging down the open road with only the moon and Mr Symes's torch for light, Josh discovered that there were more tones of black than he had thought possible. Occasionally, clouds passed across the moon's path breaking up the night sky into a patchwork of darkness. The outline of a church emerged across a field to their right. Dampness on the roof glistened as more clouds scudded across the moon leaving a silvery glow around the building.

Gazing upwards and around him, Josh began to see beauty in the night. It was less frightening than he had expected. His friend, who never seemed to sleep, shepherded them down the road. The air tasted fresh and clean. Then something flew past the couple, almost within touching distance.

'What's that?' shrieked Josh, stooping.

'Raven,' said Mr Symes.

Josh looked around trying to pick it out in the blackness but it was impossible.

Past the church, the road straightened through the countryside, only now and again passing an isolated farmhouse. Some time and very little conversation later, Josh asked the question he had been wanting to ask since they first started out.

'How far is it?'

'Three miles. Maybe four.'

'Can we have a rest soon?'

A short distance further on, they came to a stone bus shelter with a tiled roof and wooden bench where they rested and sat looking out across the fields. Clouds continued to drift across the moon and the landscape turned various shades of night. Mr Symes took out a chocolate bar from his pocket and gave it to Josh who devoured it so eagerly that he was down to the last piece before he remembered to offer some to his companion. The old man declined then spoke softly.

'Not right. Him living there.'

'What do you mean?' asked Josh.

'Mr Nathan. Stole the house he did.'

'Is that what Mrs Symes meant about you not coming into the house 'til the real owner came back?'

'Aye.'

Josh mulled over whether to tell Mr Symes what he found. How much could he trust him? He didn't even know if they were on the right road to Whitby. They hadn't seen any signs but maybe that wasn't surprising, Josh decided, given it was night. Yet he had no reason to distrust Mr Symes. And his friend, who he always trusted, had given him the encouragement to leave. *It must be right. Surely?* Josh closed his eyes and muttered under his breath. Unbeknown to Josh, Mr Symes was watching him.

'Talking to him, eh?'

Josh opened his eyes and turned to the old man. Mr Symes hesitated then looked directly at his young companion.

'Me too.'

Josh gasped and the two gazed at each other in the silent night before Mr Symes broke the stillness.

'The breeze. From the garden. Knew then.'

Josh's anxiety, which had weighed so heavily on him, floated away in the chill air. Calm seeped through him. He had never known anyone who felt the same about his friend. The connection with Mr Symes filled Josh with an unexpected freedom.

'How did you know I found something?' Josh paused. Then he realised. 'Was that you at the top of the stairs?'

The old man looked at him and nodded. Josh was relieved it had been Mr Symes and that one mystery had been explained. Mr Symes fiddled with his torch then said something that sliced through Josh as if he had been plunged into icy water.

CHAPTER 11

Where can you turn to when you're trapped?

'You're the one.'

Josh almost choked when he heard the words.

Mr Symes described how he had worked at the house since he was a boy and that Robert Haxby built the house many years ago.

'Your grandfather,' he added.

Josh turned sharply towards the old man and stared at him.

'But I haven't…mum said…'

Mr Symes took hold of Josh's arm and shuffled on the bench before replying.

'Robert Haxby knew the Prophecy. The danger. Sent all his young 'uns away soon as he found out.'

'But why did he tell you and not mum or Rupert?'

'Protect the family. Only told me on account of…' He stopped in mid sentence and changed tack but Josh didn't pick it up. 'Found out about you later.'

'Found out what about me?' Josh persisted.

'In the Prophecy. Search the kennings.'

'Kennings? That's what…' Josh stopped himself describing what Freyja, The Shield Maiden, had told him. 'What are kennings?' he continued.

'Viking words. Sort of code.'

The old man's words echoed in Josh's head and he fumbled in his rucksack for 'The Legend of Greycloak.' He took out the loose page that he had placed at the back of the book and showed it to Mr Symes.

'Like this?' he asked.

Mr Symes gulped. His eyes ran over the words but he didn't understand them.

'Aye,' he replied. 'Aye.'

'What's it mean?'

He shook his head then asked Josh where he found it. Josh explained that he'd seen a book in the study with the same writing as the loose page.

'Book?' asked Mr Symes.

'It was called 'The Bergen Prophecy.''

The old man appeared to hold his breath. Then he asked, 'Where?'

'In the study. I put it back.'

Mr Symes handed the page back to Josh.

'Shield Maiden knows,' added Mr Symes.

'The one in the painting?'

Mr Symes nodded and the image of Rachel flashed through Josh's mind again as he recalled the picture.

'And what's the white settlement?' asked Josh.

The old man glanced at him in a way adults do when they think you should know the answer to a question. Josh sighed then returned the book and the loose page to his rucksack. *Got to find out what it means.* He rocked to and fro on the bench and buried his face in his arms. A dam had burst in Josh's life and the questions kept coming with nothing to hold them back. But he needed explanations. Anything.

'What about my granddad?'

The response only added to the flood of questions.

'Said on his deathbed, a boy Haxby would return. Protector.' He paused. 'You.'

Rachel's words about being looked after and being special resounded in his head and he quizzed Mr Symes further. In a lowered voice and with his face to the ground, the old man said,

'Protect Whitby. From Greycloak.'

Josh said he had read 'The Legend of Greycloak' and repeated what Mina and Anders said about the Viking taking revenge for his father's death.

'Anyway, what's it got to do with me?' Josh asked. 'It's just a story. Isn't it?'

A flock of clouds skipped away and the moonlight exposed the despair on the old man's face.

'No story. Real.'

Josh remembered what Mr Symes said earlier.

'But why did you say I'm the one?'

The old man took some time before replying. He had never told anyone before. Mr Symes gazed out across the fields, as if looking for encouragement that what he was about to say was allowed. At that moment, a cauliflower shaped cloud sailed across the moon. The leaves of a single tree nearby rustled and the two travelling companions smiled at each other.

Josh listened to how his granddad confided in Mr Symes about the Prophecy and Greycloak's revenge. He explained that the identity of Whitby's protector would only be known just before the return of Greycloak.

'Year of the one called deliverer.'

At that moment Mr Symes stared and nodded at Josh. Then he said that the one is special and would return to the house in unusual circumstances. That was why he stared at Josh so much when he first arrived. He knew the time had come.

'Something else. A mark,' said Mr Symes.

'Uh?'

'The one. Got a mark.'

'Where?'

'Neck. Like a cross.'

Josh said he had a birthmark and turned down the collar of his top to show Mr Symes the back of his neck.

'It's not like a cross though,' said Josh.

Mr Symes took the torch from his pocket and shone it on Josh's neck. The old man gasped.

'Caedmon's cross.'

The old man explained that Caedmon lived hundreds of years ago in Whitby and that he was known as God's chosen one. He said there is a story that the one who bears the mark of Caedmon is destined for a special purpose.

'Chosen,' Mr Symes continued.

Josh sat in silence. He'd never thought much about the mark before but started to rub it as if it had some supernatural power. He was just an ordinary boy from a city estate who never wanted to go to Whitby in the first place. He would never have gone if his mum hadn't wanted him to. Or was it really her decision?

Watching the clouds gently play 'peek-a-boo' with the moon, Josh's mind was in chaos. *Why am I the last one to know about my own life?* Rachel seemed to know something and Mr Symes had just turned his life upside down. Josh couldn't help thinking that Rupert knew why he came to meet Josh off the bus. But why wasn't he saying? Did the sea have no choice but to give him up so he could achieve his destiny? And the documents in the basement? Special. The one. Someone bigger. The words flashed on and off in his mind like neon signs at the fun fair, all competing to be heard. All the fantasies that he had dreamt in his room back in Leeds seemed meaningless compared with what he was now experiencing. *And my granddad. Why didn't anyone tell me?*

An owl hooted in the distance and Josh felt the dampness of the night air on his face as they left the refuge of the bus stop. They walked through the dark but Josh was so preoccupied, churning over the recent events in his mind, that he wouldn't have noticed if they had marched through a troupe of performing acrobats. He knew he couldn't have found the way by himself and thought about the chance nature of the old man appearing when he did. *Chance?* For the first time, Josh wondered if, just maybe, there was a force guiding his life.

Some while later, they joined a main road although there was still no pavement so Josh still had to rely on Mr Symes guiding them by torchlight with the assistance of a willing moon. As the road straightened and rose slightly, Josh caught sight of a distant glint of light that grew stronger the more they walked. The nearer they got to the glow the more Josh's hopes climbed.

'The lighthouse!' exclaimed Josh.

'Aye.'

A soft gleam progressively invaded the blackness as they approached streetlights, clusters of dull, box-like buildings and a school. Within minutes, another school and the shadowy patchwork of a graveyard appeared until they were crossing a high-level road bridge above the river.

'Whitby!'

Josh ran ahead of Mr Symes and looked out from the bridge downriver towards the harbour where lights shimmered a welcome on the water. Familiar shapes of St Mary's Church, the abbey and the marina thrilled him so much that he hugged his guide. The old man was taken aback at first but then allowed himself to hug Josh back. The butterflies in Josh's stomach had stopped beating their wings and a warm stillness coursed through his body. They studied the view before them. Josh thought that night had never seemed so enchanting. So safe.

Leaving the bridge they walked down Prospect Hill towards the centre of town passing Bagdale Hall, an old building with criss crosses of grey on large rectangular windows. Previously, even in daylight, it wore a sombre expression but now, at night, this night, it offered a greeting. Josh ran ahead and leaned on the railing overlooking the marina. If he could have swept the whole of Whitby up in his arms and embraced it he would have done. The excitement of coming back charged through him like a train. It felt to Josh like coming home.

'Yeesss!' he yelled.

It didn't matter there was no one awake to hear him. The abbey knew. So did the river. He turned around to Mr Symes.

'It's like I belong here,' said Josh.

The old man's face softened into a wise old grin as he stood under a streetlight. He didn't say anything. There was no need. Josh understood. He turned towards the harbour entrance, his attention drawn by the chugging sound of a fishing boat sailing home to offload the night's catch. Mr Symes put his arm around Josh and ushered him towards the harbour. Deserted.

The sky brightened behind the abbey on the other side of the river. Although still the dark side of twilight, morning was emerging from below the horizon. Distant sounds of more fishing boat engines returning from the sea grew stronger as the two approached the pier.

'All right?' enquired Mr Symes.

'Yes. But I don't understand it all. What should I do now?' asked Josh as an afterthought.

'Tell people. Come back,' the old man pleaded, putting his hand on Josh's shoulder.

When he first went to Nathan's he never imagined that a bond could develop between him and the crusty old gardener. Yet, during the hours spent walking and talking, Josh felt a friendship growing which would last beyond that evening.

Josh struggled to know what to say. His mind was too busy processing ideas, questions and worries. Even though he didn't know how he would explain everything, he still had a deep need to talk to someone. But would anyone listen to him? Talking to his mum was impossible. And what would Rupert and Mina think? *Rachel will understand, won't she? Anders also.* Then there were the documents.

As thoughts tumbled through Josh's head Mr Symes withdrew into the darkness. Josh turned to face the oncoming light. Realising he had not even thanked him, he turned and shouted 'Thank you' into the emptiness. Gazing up at the arched whalebones he spotted two large birds circling overhead then vanishing back to the black.

Josh ambled down to the pier. Although he had been carrying his rucksack for what seemed the whole night, it didn't feel heavy; as if somebody was carrying his load for him. The air warmed and the familiar smell of diesel fuel and fish from the boats comforted him. None of the shops or cafes were open and only the fishermen, it seemed, were awake. He was alone as he walked down the pier towards the lighthouse. Josh breathed in the atmosphere of the town before making his way up to Rupert's caravan.

Sitting on a bench that surrounded the foot of the lighthouse, he watched the fish being offloaded from the boats. Piercing screeches of seagulls signalled the temptation of easy food from the cast offs thrown into the water. The blanket of the night rolled back as he thought about the way his life was changing. It was like being inside a computer game with him as the lead player.

He was so lost in his mind whirl that, at first, he didn't see two men approaching in the distant half-light. They stopped for a while and leaned on the railing looking out at the boats. As he studied the men, Josh counted seven lampposts from the start of the pier to the lighthouse. They were five lampposts away. One of them moved to the other side of the pier and gazed out at the abbey, turning occasionally to look at Josh. He clasped his rucksack tight and fidgeted on the bench. His breathing deepened and sped up the nearer they came. *Why are they on the pier so early?* It wasn't as if they had fishing tackle and they didn't have dogs that they were taking for an early morning walk.

The men walked towards each other and talked for a while before moving in Josh's direction. They were now only three lampposts away but he still didn't recognise them. It didn't look right to Josh and he wanted to get away but the approaching men, the end of the pier and the sea blocked his exit. Even if he shouted for help nobody would hear him; not even the trawlermen whose boat engines drowned out other sounds. He felt the breeze shifting around him but he didn't seem to be helping.

The sun stretched higher behind the abbey as the two men reached the nearest lamppost.

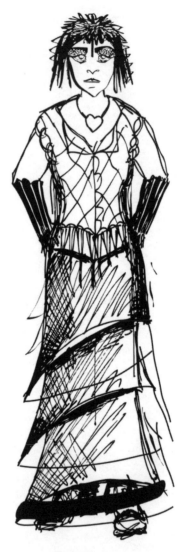

Mina

CHAPTER 12

How can you solve a puzzle without any clues?

What do they want?

Josh scrambled from the bench and thought about running down the pier. No way out. He fixed his eyes on the men and gripped his rucksack with such force that the straps dug into his hands. Josh's throat was tight. His heart thumped and his hands became clammy causing him to drop the torch. He froze and tried to yell out but panic choked his voice.

The men suddenly stopped. Seconds later, they turned and strode back towards the harbour occasionally glancing back at the slight figure still clutching his rucksack. Josh trembled and breathing was a struggle. The sun continued its climb and Josh felt his friend brushing against his face.

Josh didn't move but counted the lampposts as the men passed them. Five. Six. Seven. Then they were completely out of sight. Turning round to pick up the torch, he stumbled to the ground, looked up and yelled for all of Whitby to hear.

'Mountain!'

The man monster stood grinning, fishing rod in hand, wearing a yellow waterproof jacket and black woolly hat. He looked like a huge inflatable bee. Josh let go of his rucksack, struggled to his feet and threw himself at Mountain wrapping, as far as he could, his arms around him. Josh bounced up and down in his rescuer's arms, unable to contain his joy and relief.

115

Mountain broke into a full belly laugh that pulsated through Josh. Moments later, the reality of his situation began to sink in and tears flooded through Josh's eyes. Mountain stayed cocooning him for several minutes.

The giant and the dwarf sat watching the town wake up as the sun strengthened. Josh spoke about his time at Nathan's whilst Mountain listened in silence, nodding when appropriate.

'Do you know who those men were?' asked Josh.

Mountain shook his head.

'I missed you and the others so much,' said Josh squeezing Mountain's spade sized hand. Josh told him about 'The Bergen Prophecy', that Robert Haxby was his granddad and Mr Symes saying he was the one.

'I've got some papers in my rucksack but I don't understand them,' said Josh.

Mountain raised his eyebrows and sighed but he still kept silent.

He wanted Mountain to say something but he was grateful, nevertheless, that he was a good listener. He savoured the Whitby morning welcome and checked his pocket to see that he still had Rachel's note. Josh read it aloud to Mountain who gave him a puzzled look and held him in a great hug. Josh repeated the words until, gently, he allowed his eyes to close. The security of belonging engulfed him and he dozed off.

*

Whitby began to stir with dog walkers and people heading for work when Josh opened his eyes. Mountain picked up his fishing rod and Josh's rucksack and they ambled to 'The Dracula Experience' to see if Mina had arrived. The building was still locked. Mountain sat down in the doorway and Josh curled up alongside him to nap a while longer. He was still snoozing when Mina came to open up. She gasped when she first saw them. Mountain signalled to Mina with his finger on his lips.

'I thought Josh was at Nathan's,' she whispered. 'Is he all right?'

The sprawling giant gave a thumbs up sign just as Josh opened his eyes.

'Hiya sunshine. Welcome home.' Mina stooped down to hug Josh who clasped her tight. *Welcome home.*

'Bet you're hungry eh? Let's get you something to eat. I'll phone the café then you can tell me what's going on. Just the three bacon sandwiches?' Mina asked Mountain who grinned.

Mina unlocked the door and took them into the back room where Josh had originally found 'The Legend of Greycloak.' She phoned the café to order breakfast and made some tea.

The others ate as Josh explained how two men had followed him onto the pier but left when they saw Mountain.

'Sort of Mountain rescue then?' Mina joked.

Mountain covered his mouth and chortled. Josh looked blankly at her.

'Sorry, love. Can't help it. Us ghosts are like that.' She smiled.

Josh opened his rucksack, took out the file of documents and gave them to Mina.

'I found these. There's some funny stuff in them that might be important. We've got to tell mum and Rupert.'

'Rupert's working away today but he should be back some time this afternoon. I'll have a look then we can talk to him and see what's got you so excited.'

Mountain got up to leave and gave Josh his victory salute. Josh jumped up to hug him.

'I love you,' said Josh.

Mountain's eyes moistened and he kissed the top of Josh's

head. Mina watched them and wiped a tear that had escaped from one eye. Mountain put him down and growled playfully at his friend who growled back.

Josh was going to ask Mina why Mountain never spoke but she said something which distracted him.

'Who did Mr Symes tell you built the house?'

Josh exploded with the details of the old man's account during their night hike. Mina listened without interrupting.

Josh slumped back into his chair exhausted after he had told his story.

'You look shattered. Why don't you try and get some sleep? I'll look at these papers for a while then I must start work.'

Mina helped Josh to the faded settee. She covered Josh with his coat as he curled up and closed his eyes. The last thing he remembered was Mina humming a tune that carried him to another place.

When he awoke Mina was still sitting at the table engrossed in the papers.

'Aren't you going to work?' Josh asked in a daze.

'It's lunchtime, sleepyhead. You've been away all morning. There's a drink and a salad sandwich from Ruby with her love.'

'Oh, thanks. Do you understand those papers?'

'Before we go any further eat your sandwich. No food, no answers. Check?'

'Check,' said Josh reluctantly.

He bolted down the sandwich and drank the orange so fast that it barely touched the side of his throat.

'What's a will?' he spluttered.

'It's where a person writes saying they want to give somebody their possessions when they die. It looks as if a man called Robert Haxby...'

'He's my granddad! Mr Symes told me,' Josh cut in.

'Oh…right…anyway, it looks like he owned the house and gave it to Rupert, Nathan and your mum to share.'

'But why are mum's and Rupert's names crossed out?'

'Beats me.'

'I wish you were a real ghost. Then you'd know.'

'If I was a real ghost I'd be haunting that Beryl Stone who bullied me at school.'

'You got bullied?'

'Uuh huh. Turned out okay though haven't I? Not everyone gets to be a ghost.'

Josh laughed.

Mina shuffled through the papers scattered on the table.

'There's this letter to a solicitor…and it looks as if the will was changed so Nathan got everything and your mum and Rupert got nothing.'

'What about where someone's written the same name loads of times?'

She screwed up her face and sighed deeply.

'What? What?'

'I'd say somebody was practising a signature.'

'Why would they do that?'

Mina shook her head but said nothing.

The more answers Josh got, the less he understood. Frustrated, he slouched back in his chair. So many things seemed out of place and he couldn't piece them together. Even Mina couldn't work them out.

'Maybe Rupert will have a better idea,' she said.

Josh returned to the conversation he had with Mr Symes the night before.

'Why did Mr Symes say I'm the one?'

'He's probably just a bit confused.'

'But he said I've got a special mark. On my neck. Look.'

He rolled down the collar of his top and showed Mina his birthmark. Something about it jolted her.

'It looks like…'

'Mr Symes said it looks like a…cross thing.'

'Caedmon's cross,' she said.

If Mina had been uncertain about Josh's story before, the revelation about his birthmark made her think again. Her face, which previously had been gentle and relaxed, suddenly hardened. Josh tensed up and wondered whether he had done anything wrong. Mina stood up and walked around the room, twiddling the rings on her fingers.

'You know I said before about this Viking who's meant to stalk the town, well I've heard people talk about some prophecy that…'

'It's the Bergen Prophecy. Anders told me and Mr Symes said ask the Shield Maiden.'

'Tell me again what Mr Symes said. The bit about Greycloak and you being the one.'

Josh repeated what the old man had told him. The more he retold the story the more bewildered he became about what was happening to him. Mina put her arm around him and held him close.

'Always remember that you're special. Whether you're the one, as Mr Symes puts it, or just good old Josh Haxby.'

'Rachel said someone was looking after me.'

'I think she's right. Somebody greater than you and me.'

Josh leaned his head on her shoulder and stared into space. His thoughts kept boomeranging back to Anders' story about the man in Bergen. Although he knew the adults were trying to understand, and Rachel appeared to know more, he couldn't wait to tell Anders everything. *I've got to see him.*

*

M.ountain

Mina and Josh were still talking as Rupert arrived at 'The Dracula Experience' later that day. When he appeared, Josh flung himself at his uncle and hugged him so tight that he almost knocked Rupert off his feet. They swayed together in a close embrace whilst Mina looked on, smiling.

As Josh recounted his story, his uncle read the documents in an increasingly agitated state. Although he was interested in what Josh had said about Greycloak, his attention was drawn more to the unfolding possibility that Nathan had obtained the house falsely and tricked his brother and sister out of their inheritance. Rupert's face tightened but he held back from saying too much when Mina cast a sideways glance at him.

'I don't have to go back to Nathan's do I?'

'Of course not. Don't worry, we'll get it sorted,' said Rupert.

Josh fidgeted on the settee then asked the question that had burned bright in is mind since his talk with Mr Symes.

'Why didn't anyone tell me about my granddad?'

Rupert sat back and looked at Mina who tilted her head towards him.

'It's a long story,' said Rupert.

'I don't care! I want to know!'

His uncle was taken aback by Josh's insistence but Mina covered her face suppressing a smile. Josh saw his reaction and thought perhaps he had overstepped the mark so he slouched back in his chair and looked down at the floor.

'Your mum should really tell you but since she's not here I guess it's up to me. She'll probably kill me for saying but…'

Josh sat upright, expectant, hopeful that his determination had paid off and he would get at least one answer to the riddles teasing him. Rupert settled down for what Josh hoped would be a detailed explanation.

'When your mum and me were young, very young…'

'What about Nathan?' Josh interrupted.

'Yes and him but he's the least of my worries. Anyhow, we were sent to live with an aunt…'

'In Leeds?'

'This is going to take a long time if you keep jumping in every five seconds.'

'Sorry.'

'It's okay. I understand that you want to know. So we went to live in Leeds…'

Rupert explained how their father, Robert Haxby, sent them away because he didn't like having children around. At least that's what they were told. Their mother had died when she gave birth to Josh's mum who was the youngest of the three. As they grew up, none of the children wanted anything more to do with their father.

'Why did you come back to Whitby then?' asked Josh.

'The sea. Always loved it. Then a friend of mine offered me a job so it all fitted.'

'Mr Symes told me granddad sent you away to protect you.'

'Protect us? From what?'

Mina, who until now had listened quietly, shuffled uneasily in her chair.

"The Bergen Prophecy." It's at Nathan's house but I've got a page of it,' added Josh taking it from his rucksack to show them. 'The rest is in the study. Nathan told me not to go in there but I did. I couldn't read it properly because it was all wavy writing. But I know where it is.'

'If we could get it, we could check out whether Mr Symes was right about your father. And Greycloak,' Mina continued.

'We could get it now.' Josh sprang out of his seat, ready to leave at once.

'Easy, tiger, we'll have to be careful how we do this.'

Rupert considered all the evidence before him. Even he was reeling from the news about the reason for his father sending his three children away. Everything he had believed for so many years had been turned inside out.

'Sorry, boys, I really must finish up here. Leave your rucksack, Josh and I'll fetch it up later. Okay?' Mina gave them both a kiss on the cheek and rushed out of the door.

'I've got to tell Anders,' said Josh taking the loose page from 'The Bergen Prophecy' with him.

Rupert gathered up the remaining papers and told Josh to meet him back at the caravan at half past six. Then Rupert gave him a reassuring hug and smile before leaving.

Despite all the evidence that was stacking up in front of him, Josh still couldn't take the final step to believing. Maybe it was all a coincidence. Part of him didn't want to believe any of it, yet at every turn, he found himself being sucked back into a whirlpool of maybes. *What if it's true?*

*

Josh ran to Kristjan's, swerving through the crowds strolling by the riverside. When he arrived he barged through the restaurant doors. As usual, there were no customers, only Kristjan, alone at the back cleaning glasses. He looked up expectantly when he heard the doors open.

'Josh! You back?'

'Where's Anders? I need to speak to him,' panted Josh.

'On pier. Fishing. You okay?'

'Yes, thanks.'

Josh turned on the spot and bolted out. He galloped down the road scattering a group of seagulls who were idling their time away in a large puddle. Past boats that were out of the water, resting on large wooden supports on the quayside, looking as if they were flying through the air. 'Sea Jay', 'Pride and Joy', 'Kindly Light', 'Beakey' and 'Samurai', each with their names written in a distinct style and their hulls painted in brilliant blues, yellows and reds. He tore down the road and weaved in and out of the lampposts on the pier until he reached the end.

Before he got to their favourite fishing spot, Josh saw Anders sauntering towards him with his fishing tackle slung over his shoulders.

'I knew you were coming,' Anders called out, emerging from a group of people fishing at the end of the pier. He lurched towards Josh who sped to greet him. It had been almost two weeks since Josh had left but it seemed as if they had never been apart.

'I've got loads to tell you.' Josh was still recovering from running.

'Let's go back to the restaurant. My father made krumkake this morning.'

'Krumkake? Yes! I've really missed your dad's baking.'

Josh thought about his mum and felt a twinge of guilt that Kristjan's cooking had taken over from his mum's in his thoughts. He helped Anders carry his fishing tackle back to the restaurant. They talked non-stop.

Although excited at seeing his best friend again, Josh still couldn't help wondering why Anders was in a T-shirt and shorts in spite of it being windy on the pier. Especially when everyone else was wearing kagouls and hats. Even when it got cold, Anders didn't need extra clothing. *It's not normal.*

*

Josh garbled his story and repeated Mr Symes's words in between mouthfuls of food. As he revealed further details, Anders became more animated whilst Kristjan looked down at the floor. When Josh mentioned the grey Viking and the two birds that seemed to follow him, Kristjan suddenly looked up.

'Not good,' he said shaking his head.

'I knew, I knew. It's not just a story. That weird man in Bergen who kept watching us.'

When Josh showed them the kenning from 'The Bergen Prophecy', Kristjan got up and returned to polishing the glasses. The worry was imprinted on his face.

'Careful who you talk,' said Kristjan. 'I cook scrumbie. Customers tonight, maybe. Good seeing you, Josh.' Kristjan slipped away into the kitchen.

'Scrumbie? What's that?' asked Josh.

'Herring. He gets it fresh from the boats and cooks it a really good way.'

'Will you have any customers tonight?'

'Don't think so but he always cooks something. Just in case.'

Josh asked Anders why his dad looked so worried. Anders explained that the man in Bergen was the real reason they had come to Whitby.

'What Mr Symes told you made him remember.'

'Do you think that man you saw in Bergen really was…?' Josh couldn't bring himself to finish his sentence.

Anders studied the words of the kenning in silence for a while.

'Do you know what it means?' asked Josh.

'I've seen stuff like this in books but never a real one. I think it's some sort of code.'

Because the writing was peculiar, Anders read the words slowly, precisely and aloud in order to make them out.

ON THE FIRST AND TWENTY SUN RISING
OF THE WINTER BRINGING MANUOR OF GOR
ON THE DAY OF TIW THE SON-SLAYER
BLOOD RIVERS AND DWELLING WRECKAGE
WILL RIDE ON THE STORM STEEDS ACROSS THE SAIL ROAD
TO THE WHITE SETTLEMENT
FROM THE KINGDOM OF THE GREYCLOAK
THIS WILL GIVE BIRTH IN THE YEAR OF THE FATHERLESS
   ONE
WHOSE NAME IS DELIVERER

'Mr Symes said ask the Shield Maiden. And there's a painting of Freyja the Shield Maiden at Nathan's house. Who is she?'

Anders explained that, in Viking legends, Freyja was a powerful lady who kept people safe.

'But when I looked at the painting I kept seeing…'

Josh didn't finish his sentence but sighed in frustration and slumped forward on the table with his head in his hands.

Anders continued studying the words. After some time his face lit up.

'If you put… these words together…then see what…'

Josh watched as Anders began to find some meaning in the riddle.

'First and twenty…that's the twenty first, I suppose…and sun rising is… day maybe, so…'

'Twenty first of what, though?' queried Josh. 'What's manuor of gor?'

'I don't know but if it says winter bringing then maybe it's to do with…the start of winter,' said Anders.

The boys slouched backwards and looked at each other, baffled by the words. Another road blocked. Dead end. Again.

With Anders examining the kenning further, Josh paced

around the restaurant fiddling with the salt and pepper pots on the tables. Visions of the painting of Freyja the Shield Maiden interchanged with Rachel in Josh's head. Then he stopped dead. The sudden change in his behaviour caused Anders to look up.

'What?'

'We'll ask Rachel,' said Josh. 'She knows things.'

Anders gave the page back to Josh. Even though they didn't speak, the boys became aware that their futures, unfolding before them, were becoming entwined and that they were at the beginning of a long journey which was taking them…where? They stared out of the window at the slate grey clouds ghosting in from the sea. Josh turned to leave but Anders grasped his arm and, without speaking, pointed to the cliff top by St Mary's church. A Viking warrior in deepest grey stood alone amongst the tombstones, holding a large triangular shaped banner. The banner displayed a black bird with wings spread wide. *It's like those birds I keep seeing.*

'Let's check him out,' said Anders, his voice crackling with enthusiasm.

Josh held him back and shook his head.

Turning over thoughts of Greycloak, the Shield Maiden and the kenning in his head, Josh still couldn't work out how he and Anders fitted into the puzzle. It was like trying to put together a jigsaw in the dark; unable to see the images and having to feel the pieces together.

The warrior dissolved into the gloom.

Rover

CHAPTER 13

Do animals understand when you talk to them?

With the parts of the puzzle still refusing to fit together and the image of the warrior haunting his mind, Josh went to the kitchen. Kristjan was gutting herring and casting the heads and bones into a large black bin. The fish eyes, dark and dead, seemed to focus on Josh as he watched the knife slicing through the pearly-coated flesh. Kristjan didn't look up but continued with his work. Josh regretted hurting Kristjan by bringing back memories he hoped he had left behind in Norway.

'Rachel says someone's looking after us. Somebody bigger and more powerful than anything.' He struggled to reassure Kristjan.

'Maybe.' Kristjan was not cheered by Josh's words but managed a half smile.

'Thanks for the krumkake. They're the best.'

'Tell friends eh?' Kristjan wrapped up some herring he had filleted and gave it to Josh.

'For tea.'

Josh thanked him and smiled broadly. 'Rachel knows about these things. She does.'

'She sound nice lady. I meet one day huh?'

*

Josh dawdled back along the quayside towards Rupert's caravan, wrestling with the change happening to his life. He had stepped off the lazy train to normality onto a roller coaster. He had no way of knowing whether he would ever step back into his previous world or if he had passed through a one-way door.

He threaded his way up Church Street, through the crowds, towards the one hundred and ninety nine stone steps littered with people catching their breath from the steep climb. Drizzle saturated his clothes and he grew more anxious as he approached St Mary's church where the Viking had appeared. His heart beat faster the higher he climbed. By the time he had got to the top of the steps the jealous sun had broken through the clouds and beamed down on Josh from a clearing blue sky. There was no sign of the grey warrior so his breathing eased. A metallic dampness hung heavy in the thick air.

A bank of haze rolled back across the sea. Lights, similar to burning torches, glowed in the murkiness and, as he looked closer, he saw outlines of Viking ships that appeared to hover above the water. The warrior stood at the bow of the lead ship. Even though the air had warmed, Josh still shivered at the images that nobody else appeared to notice. *Why can't they see?* He continued past the abbey but when he glanced back, the ships and the menacing haze had vanished.

The landscape brightened as Josh strode alongside the Yorkshire stone wall leading to the gates of the caravan park. Perched on the post box outlined against a lush green field was Rover, in the same position as he had been when Josh left for Nathan's. It seemed as if he was waiting for Josh. He darted up to Rover who padded towards him meowing.

'I've missed you so much.' Josh picked him up and held him tight nuzzling into his moist fur. He carried him to the caravan but Rover became more interested in the herring that Josh had in his pocket.

Spotting Rupert's motorbike parked outside, Josh ran the last few metres and hurtled up the steps to the front door. Mina and Rupert were sitting drinking tea when Josh burst through. They got up to welcome him and all the worry and tension flooded out of him at the reality of being back with people he loved. Josh clung to Rupert with one arm and held Rover tight with the other. The familiar smell of Rupert's biker gear and the views from the window reassured Josh in spite of all the upheaval in his life.

'Welcome back, Josh. Hey, you're all soggy.'

'Soggy moggy by the looks of it as well,' said Mina kissing Josh's head before fetching a towel.

Rover was going frantic attempting to get to the herring in Josh's pocket.

'Better get out of those wet clothes. Your rucksack's in your room. Phew!' Rupert winced. 'Have you been down the fish market?'

'Kristjan gave me some herring for tea.'

He took the fish out of his pocket and gave it to Mina.

'I'll cook it and you get changed. You'd better let Rover have some or you may lose a friend.'

'They told me about the man in Bergen, that's in Norway, and Freyja, she's a Shield Maiden and…'

'Okay, okay. Get sorted out and you can tell us over tea. It's great to have you back.'

Josh grinned, gave Rupert and Mina another hug and went to his room to change into dry clothes. He dried his hair with a towel and took his beloved photo from his rucksack. Kissing the picture of his mum, he put it back by the window then hung up the wind chime. He opened the window, smiled and talked to his friend who sailed through, tinkling a soothing melody on the chimes.

Josh finished his tea whilst Rover, who had already devoured his share of the herring, studied Josh's every move. There was a knock at the door.

'That'll be Rachel,' said Rupert.

'Rachel?' Josh sprang off his chair and flew through the door, all but knocking her off her feet.

'Hey, lad.' Rachel clung to him and kissed him as they stood in the damp air. 'I said I'd see you later.'

The two were still hugging each other as they moved inside.

'We thought Rachel should hear your story,' said Mina, fetching an extra mug.

Josh talked late into the night whilst a buttery moon warmed the darkness. He turned towards his bedroom door when he heard his wind chime sounding. He smiled and Rachel touched his hand as if she understood.

'Where are these papers then?' asked Rachel.

Mina fetched them from the dining table and passed them to her.

'And there's a strange book with weird writing and stuff but it's still at Nathan's house,' said Josh apologetically. 'It said 'The Bergen Prophecy' on the inside.'

'I need to see that.'

Rachel's curiosity increased and she held Josh's hand sensing his unease.

Josh ran back into his bedroom to get the loose page he kept in the back of 'The Legend of Greycloak.' When he returned he showed it to Rachel. She studied it for a while then nodded to herself.

'What's it mean?' implored Josh.

'Kennings,' she replied, running her hand across the page. The others watched with curiosity before Josh exclaimed,

'That's what the painting…,' but Josh stopped in mid sentence.

Rachel touched his arm then read the words to herself, whispering 'October.'

Rupert and Mina cast glances between each other and Josh gave her a bewildered look before adding,

'Mr Symes said the Shield Maiden knows.'

'Did he now?' said Rachel.

As the adults talked, Josh studied Rachel, observing her movements and mannerisms. She always seemed so calm and he wondered if she ever got upset. Occasionally she turned to Josh and winked at him. His thoughts jumped back to the painting of the Shield Maiden Freyja at Nathan's house. In his mind, the two separate images of Rachel and Freyja appeared to blend into one. His head was a jumble of ideas and pictures that were impossible to make sense of or put into order.

'Rachel?' asked Rupert. 'Could you take these papers to the police first thing tomorrow? I think I'll go up to Nathan's house but I need to know these are safe.'

'No problem but you can do me a favour too. Get that book will you?'

'If I can find it.' Rupert glanced at Josh. 'You'll have to tell me where it is.'

'I'll show you when we get there,' Josh enthused.

'No, you'd better stay here.'

'I'm not telling you where it is unless I can come,' he insisted.

Rachel folded her arms and admired Josh's blossoming courage. Mina sat back in her chair, nodded and grinned at Josh. Rupert looked around at everyone and sighed, recognising he was outnumbered and would be wasting his time protesting.

'Okay, but no running off doing your own thing.' Rupert fixed his gaze on Josh so that his nephew was in no doubt.

'As if,' said Rachel, stroking Josh's hair. The youngest person in the room smirked contentedly, realising the power this information had given him.

Rachel gathered the papers together then turned to Josh and held his hand.

'Something for you. Been waiting for the right person to give it to. Reckon I've found him now.'

She took a small packet from the inside of her brown leather jacket and unwrapped the tissue paper as if it was a religious ceremony. The unfurled sheets revealed a silver cross and chain that gave off an extraordinary glow even though there was no light reflecting on it.

'Look familiar?' said Rachel to Josh's surprise.

'It's…it's like the shape of my birthmark and the cross in the churchyard.' Josh's stare was intense.

'The cross of Caedmon. It's yours now.'

Rachel took the cross and placed it around Josh's neck.

'Always wear it, lad. You'll see why soon enough.'

'But why are you giving it to me?'

'It was made for you.'

The look on Josh's face showed his confusion. He examined the cross in between glances at Rachel. Rupert appeared mystified but Mina remained watchful throughout. Her expression implied that she understood the impact on Josh. At least in part.

'Remember this,' said Rachel. 'Only two other people must ever be allowed to hold the cross.'

'Who's that?'

'You'll know.'

Whenever Josh received an answer, it only posed another question. *How will I know?* Rachel got up to leave.

'Anders made a sign of the cross to me,' said Josh. Rachel smiled at him and held the side of his face in one hand.

'Thanks, Rachel. See you at the café tomorrow?' said Rupert.

'Depends. Ruby said there's a problem with the building. Safety stuff. Tell us how it goes at Nathan's.'

She looked straight at Josh.

'I'll get it.'

It was late when Josh got to bed. In spite of his long night walk and all he had gone through he never slept. Too much had happened over the last few days to make sense of and the unanswered questions were piling up.

As he lay in bed, the curtains open so he could see the lighthouse, there were some truths he held onto amongst all the uncertainties. He was back amongst people who cared for him. The lighthouse shone what ever the weather. His friend stirred outside and his mum looked at him from the photo propped up by the window. Rover lay on the chair purring whilst Josh talked to him constantly about who might share the cross with him. He rolled over in bed and studied the kenning. First and twenty. White settlement. *Rachel said October. That's soon.* The more he looked at the kenning the denser seemed the mystery surrounding it. He put the page down and thought about Rachel. *She knows.*

*

Josh got up early, his mind still buzzing. When he got to the front door he saw that the postman had already been and some letters were scattered on the floor. As he picked them up he noticed one item, a card, which made him laugh and his spirit leap. It was a picture of the Swedish chef from the Muppets show making popcorn. Josh turned it over and yelled with delight when he saw that it was addressed to him from his mum. All it said was 'Love you, mum' with a whole row of kisses and a hand drawn picture of Josh getting messed up with flour from the baking. His eyes welled up with joy tears. Kissing the picture, he placed it in his bedroom alongside his photo.

Rover had wandered off, Rupert was still asleep and the previous day's rain had vanished leaving a bright, clear dawn. Josh went outside to look for Rover. He felt the dew under his feet and smelled the fading dampness as the warmth of the day started to take hold. Walking around the caravan park, he found the cat sitting on his favourite spot on a wall.

'I've got to get that book for Rachel. Do you think it's important?'

The cat opened his eyes wide, stared intently at Josh for a while then narrowed them.

'Okay, so it's important. What about this cross? Who do you think I should share it with?' Rover adopted a tea cosy like pose, shut his eyes and curled up to sleep.

'Oh, thanks,' Josh moaned.

Slouching against the wall, Josh gazed at the abbey where the rising sun changed the tone of the ruins from a dreary ash colour to a gleaming gold. He wished the sun could do the same for his mum. *Why didn't she say if she was getting better?*

Thinking ahead about the journey to the house, Josh agonised over Nathan's reaction to him and whether 'The Bergen Prophecy' would still be where he left it.

CHAPTER 14

Can imagination become real?

Rupert and Josh walked down to Mina's cottage perched on the hillside overlooking the river. From there she drove the three of them to Nathan's house in her rusty blue Volkswagen Beetle. Josh sat on the back seat watching the scenery flow by. He thought about his mum. For a moment he thought he saw her smiling face looking at him in the driver's rear view mirror but the image evaporated when Mina saw him watching her.

'All right, sunshine?' she asked.

'Yes, thanks.'

Retracing the route he had taken previously with Nathan seemed odd but this time Josh knew he wouldn't be staying long. The anxiety he felt previously was now replaced by confidence and determination. Clouds bubbled up from the sea obscuring the sun as they approached Nathan's house but from the sway of the trees Josh could see his friend was with him. They turned into the leaf-shrouded driveway and trundled up to the front door, passing Mr Symes who was pruning some bushes. The old man stopped working when he noticed Josh in the back seat waving and grinning at him. He waved back, nodded then returned to his work.

Mina parked in front of the house and the three got out, standing motionless for a short while.

'Bit small isn't it?' she joked gawping at the size of the house.

Rupert took two deep breaths and led the others up the front steps. Mrs Symes opened the door.

'Where you get to then?' said Mrs Symes to Josh. 'Mr Nathan's been worried sick.'

'It's him we've come to see,' said Rupert.

Nathan appeared from his study and stood behind his housekeeper.

'It's all right, Mrs Symes. I saw them coming. That will be all.' She hesitated, shook her head, tutted then returned to the kitchen. Nathan glared at Josh then continued.

'Your mother won't be pleased. Get your things and put them up in your room. And keep it tidier in future!'

'I'm not coming back,' Josh objected, sidling up to Mina.

'We need to talk,' said Rupert. 'About some papers Josh found here.'

'I don't know what you mean,' Nathan protested. 'But if Josh has been going where he shouldn't he needs to do some explaining.'

'Rachel's taken them to the police!' Josh blurted out.

Mina put her hand on Josh's shoulder. Nathan's face turned pasty. He tried to slink away into the study but the others followed. Josh was going to fetch 'The Bergen Prophecy' from the desk but his attention was diverted by the conversation. Rupert pressed Nathan further about their father's will.

'Your vivid imagination will get you into serious trouble, young man,' Nathan insisted.

'Who were those men who chased me on the pier?' Josh protested.

'No, no, no. They weren't chasing you. When Mrs Symes found you weren't in your room I asked some people to start looking for you.'

'I don't believe you!' yelled Josh.

Mina stood still, her arms folded in front of her, fixing Nathan with a stare. Rupert pushed Nathan hard for an explanation of the papers Josh had found. The longer the conversation went on, the more Nathan wriggled like a worm on a fishing line as he attempted to deny he was guilty of any offence. Josh believed that Nathan had done something wrong but was unsure exactly what. He listened to his uncles arguing then broke in.

'Mr Symes said you don't own this house. He told me.'

'You shouldn't listen to a confused old man. Of course I own the house.'

'Prove it,' said Rupert.

'Ah…well…I expect the solicitors have got all the details.'

Rupert and Josh hounded Nathan with questions that he found difficult to answer.

'Did you fake that will, Nathan?'

'How ridiculous.'

'How come you got the house to yourself, then?'

Nathan looked down at the floor, shuffling nervously from foot to foot. Before Rupert could ask anything more, Mrs Symes skulked into the study.

'Sorry, Mr Nathan. Two policemen are at the door. They want to talk to you.'

Nathan's face started to twitch as he left the room followed by Mrs Symes. Mina put her arm round Josh whilst Rupert, hands in pockets, wandered around the room.

Several minutes later, Mrs Symes returned in a very agitated state.

'They've taken Mr Nathan away. What's going to happen to us now?' she complained. Mina took her by the arm and gestured to her to sit down.

Rupert told Mrs Symes what Josh had found in the basement and that the papers indicated Nathan had forged his father's will to keep everything for himself.

'Knew it.' Mr Symes appeared at the door.

'Mr Symes! But I thought you said you'd never come inside

until…the real…' Josh's words tailed off as the significance of what he was saying crackled through his mind. Then he recalled the time Mr Symes appeared that night he left for Whitby. The sun broke through the gloom outside and cast a shaft of light through the window into the study. Everything seemed to stop. Josh looked around at the adults who appeared still, like waxworks in a museum.

Rupert was the first to speak.

'We'll have to sell the house.'

'But why?' demanded Josh. 'We could all live here.'

Mina brushed Josh's face with the back of her hand and Rupert made a playful jab at Josh's arm.

'We can't let Mr and Mrs Symes be thrown out,' Josh objected. 'Mr Symes helped me get back.'

Noticing the worry in Mr Symes's eyes and the pleading look that Josh was giving Rupert, Mina held Josh close to reassure him.

'But the house is important. It's got a destiny hasn't it, Mr Symes?'

Mr Symes nodded in agreement.

'You and your destiny,' said Rupert.

Josh repeated what Mr Symes had said on their night walk but his words left Rupert even more confused. Mina kept silent but her look suggested there might be some truth in what they were saying. Mrs Symes cradled her head in her hands, sobbing, unaware of the conversation around her.

'Well…maybe you could stay here for a while,' Rupert agreed. 'At least until we know about the will.'

'That could be a long time, couldn't it?' said Josh.

'I guess so.'

Josh moved towards Mr Symes.

'It'll be all right. Rachel says all things work together to those who love.'

Mr Symes helped his wife up from the chair and guided her

back to the kitchen. Rupert followed them out.

'Can I ask you something about my father…?' asked Rupert.

Josh watched them leave then remembered.

'The book. I have to get the book.'

He ran over to the desk, rolled up the front and unlocked the internal drawer with the key from the small tray.

'I've got it!' he yelled, waving it in the air.

'Well done, you.'

Josh beamed and held 'The Bergen Prophecy' close to his chest, relieved it was still there and that he had worried for no reason.

Mina walked back into the hall gazing at the interior. She stopped suddenly and tilted her head to one side as if she was listening to something.

'Can you hear it too?' asked Josh.

She shook her head and sighed.

'It's probably just my imagination,' she replied.

Rupert emerged some while later from his conversation with Mr Symes. He seemed distracted so Mina put her arm around Rupert and escorted him to the car. Josh followed then turned back to look at the house that was different now Nathan had gone and Mr Symes had finally come inside. On the journey to Rupert's caravan, Josh clung to the book. At first he didn't want to open it, almost afraid that words might escape from it. But the pull was too strong. Within a few minutes, Josh opened it and thumbed through the pages to see if there were any words that stood out amongst the fancy lettering. Then three words stole his breath.

When they arrived back, Rupert and Mina got out but Josh was lost in the book and didn't move from the back seat. Mina glanced at Rupert and nodded her head in the direction of the caravan leaving Josh staring at the words. *Cross of Caedmon.*

CHAPTER 15

Do some people see things that others can't?

Josh slept fitfully that night. He got up early to visit Rachel at her cottage and to show her 'The Bergen Prophecy'. Her reaction took him aback. He had expected her to be pleased, but instead, she showed little reaction.

'What's wrong?'

'Sorry, love. No, you did well.'

She ran her hands over the book and sighed deeply. He watched her as she moved over to the window and stared into the distance. She muttered several words that sounded like a foreign language, similar to the one he had heard Kristjan speak occasionally. She turned towards Josh.

'How's about you and me having a special breakfast at the café? If it's still there.'

The thought of a Rachel sized breakfast of bacon, eggs, mushrooms and tomatoes would normally have had Josh's taste buds popping but her mood sapped the fizz out of them.

*

The café was empty when they arrived, except for Banjo, who sat alone with a mug of tea and a bowl of porridge, laced golden by the syrup he had poured onto it.

'Full works please, love. Twice!' Rachel called to Ruby who raised a strained smile. 'You all right, love?' she continued. Ruby shook her head. Josh ran over to Banjo expecting his usual, crazy greeting but instead he got silence. Banjo kept on stirring his porridge until the golden syrup had turned the oats a pale honey tone. Rachel and Josh sat down next to him but he kept staring into his breakfast.

'What's the matter with everyone this morning?'

Banjo stopped playing with his food and lolled back in his chair.

'Eh? Oh…it's closing. Like terminator.'

'What's closing?' asked Josh.

'This place. There's a notice on the wall by the counter,' continued Banjo.

Rachel ambled over to the counter where a hand written notice read:

BECAUSE OF THE UNSAFE NATURE OF THE BUILDING THE COUNCIL HAVE ORDERED THAT THE CAFÉ CLOSE FROM TONIGHT INDEFINITELY. SORRY. THANKS TO ALL OUR CUSTOMERS.

'No way,' said Josh.

Ruby shook her head and, with misty eyes, returned to preparing what would be their last breakfast in the café. The salty aroma of crispy bacon filled the place as they ate in silence but their appetites had shrunk and it took longer than normal to finish. Josh looked up at Banjo then said,

'Don't forget, Banjo. All things work together to those who love.'

'Yeah, far out. What?' He looked at Josh and knitted his eyebrows but Rachel curled her arm around Josh and kissed him firmly on the cheek.

'You're learning, lad,' she said. Rachel and Josh winked at each other in unison.

*

Josh sloped back to the caravan. He wanted to tell Rupert about the café but his uncle had left a note saying he was visiting Josh's mum at the hospital to explain recent events. He poured himself a glass of water and settled down at the table to write a letter to his mum on an exercise pad he found in the kitchen drawer.

It took Josh most of the morning to write the letter. He became sidetracked watching seagulls hovering in mid air, daydreaming and talking to Rover. Josh kept asking him what to write but Rover showed only occasional interest between bouts of sleeping and rolling over on his back to have his tummy rubbed. He knew Rupert would explain everything to his mum but Josh still wanted to tell her himself. Writing the letter made it feel like he was talking to her and helped him try to make sense of it all. He thought about 'The Bergen Prophecy' and whether he should never have started to read it. Josh thought about his granddad and how he was involved in the whole affair. His mind was a kaleidoscope of images and ideas as he started to write.

Dear mum,

I'm really really sorry I haven't written to you. Everything's been mad and there's so much to tell you. I hope you're getting better.

I so want to see you. When can I come and see you? I hope it's soon.

Don't be angry but I'm still at Rupert's. Nathan's been arrested because he did something wrong with a will. He doesn't own the house by himself. You and Rupert own it as well.

I went to stay at Nathan's later but I found these papers which I took to Mina cos she's Rupert's girlfriend and nobody else was around except Mountain who rescued me from two men who chased me on the pier after Mr Symes took me back to Whitby.

And I've got a brilliant new friend called Anders from Norway and his dad owns a restaurant and makes great krumkake. They're like rolled up cakes with cream but you'd make better ones. You'd like it here.

Rachel knows lots of stuff and she's great and she told me I'm special cos I've got a destiny. So did Mr Symes. He said a man called Greycloak's not dead and he's coming back to Whitby and York to take revenge and I'm the one but it's all mixed up and I keep seeing weird things that other people can't see. I wish I could talk to you. Rover tries his best but he only opens his eyes and flicks his tail. He's a cat.

Rupert says I don't need to call him Uncle any more and he's very kind really he is. The holidays will be over soon and I want to see you a lot. I really, really love you.

Josh XxXxXxXxX

He drew a picture of Rover on the letter and showed it to him.

'Do you think it looks like you?'

Rover glowered at Josh, narrowing his eyes and yawning before going back to sleep. Josh folded the letter and slid it into an envelope. He didn't know the hospital address so he left it standing against the biscuit tin in the kitchen, ready for Rupert to take on his next visit. His mind wouldn't let go of one question. *Why me?*

*

Although it was lunchtime he wasn't hungry. His breakfast had been enough to feed him for the whole day. He walked over to the abbey. Rover kept him company for a while but then became distracted by a bird hopping along the cliff side and pranced over to investigate. By the time Josh arrived amongst the ruins the sun was so high that his shadow had virtually disappeared.

Dawdling through the abbey grounds Josh saw Anders sitting by one of the grizzled columns, throwing a football high into the air in front of him and diving to catch it. Josh raced over to him.

'I thought you'd come,' said Anders. 'We think the same, don't we?'

Grinning, Josh nodded then asked,

'You know when you made the sign of the cross to me?'

Anders stopped juggling the football and looked solemn.

'What did you mean?' Josh continued.

Anders explained it was a sign of protection that the people of Bergen used whenever anyone mentioned the name of Harald Greycloak. Josh showed him the cross and chain which Rachel gave him. The effect of the sun made it even more dazzling.

'Wow!'

'Rachel says there's only two other people in the world I can share this with.' Josh paused and looked straight at Anders. 'I want you to be one of them but I don't know who else.'

Josh smiled feebly then looked away into the distance. He put the cross back in his pocket.

'What's the matter?' asked Anders.

'I don't know. Something seems…weird. Can't you feel it?'

'What?'

Josh looked down at the ground and picked some grass that

he rolled between his fingers. Anders put his hand on his friend's shoulder and said,

'Sometimes I've been really scared then it's okay in the end. Didn't Rachel say we're being looked after anyway?'

Josh looked up, his smile more reassured. He took out the piece of paper from Rachel that he carried with him everywhere and read it out.

'All things work together to those who love. That's what Rachel says.'

Josh mulled over what he had said and added,

'Maybe, if it helps…but we don't know why….it's still okay.'

At that moment Josh's friend blew in and playfully swept some leaves into their faces.

'See?'

They pushed each other over and fell around, laughing.

They lay on the ground watching the sky, which began to shift and change tone. Anders said how fantastic it was that they were such great friends but Josh wasn't paying attention. He had got back up and was concentrating on everything around him. Although he couldn't see anything unusual his instincts told him otherwise. Josh looked back up at the sky as ash coloured clouds stained the blue. He stared out to sea and saw shapes with lights like flames but he couldn't work out exactly what they were. He rubbed his eyes and when he looked again they were still there. Closer. Slowly, their identity became clearer. Ships. The distant sky dimmed to an unnatural grey as the clouds deepened, exploding with thunder and streaking with flashes of lightning.

Anders noticed Josh pacing around.

'What's up?'

Josh sat back down on the grass.

'I keep seeing things,' he said. 'My eyes must be funny.'

Anders told him it was because he watched too much Dr

Who. He threw a handful of grass over Josh who watched the sky closing in around them.

'I feel cold. Don't you?' asked Josh.

Anders shook his head.

Unconcerned by the invading chill, Anders ran over to retrieve his football. It had rolled away when they were larking about and was nestling against a ruined wall. As he turned around his face drained of colour and emotion. He froze. The army of swelling clouds, which had spirited in from the sea, crashed above them, veiling the sun and releasing a creeping mist. An oppressive metallic odour weighed heavy in the air.

'What is it, Anders?'

Josh's voice trembled. He got up and followed Anders' line of vision beyond the abbey grounds towards the cliff edge. Neither of them moved nor spoke. It was as if the air had been sucked out and everything had been paralysed, making it difficult for the boys to breathe. All movement had stopped. No birds flew. Life suspended. Except.

CHAPTER 16

Why do bad things sometimes happen?

A figure, blurred at first, approached them through the clinging fog. Then more shapes. The hum of low, rhythmic chanting in an unknown language echoed around them. When they were less than one hundred metres away the images in the background stopped. The angry sky twisted and groaned.

Gradually, the boys saw the image more clearly, as if they were focusing through a camera lens. Everything about him was grey. They wanted to run but an unseen force prevented them. The man approached. Nearer now. Until he stopped in the middle of the abbey grounds. Shield. Sword. Unmistakeable. *Viking*.

Without warning, he raised his cloak-draped arms and two birds appeared from nowhere swooping down low over the boys. Screeching. Near enough for them to feel the surge of wings on their faces. Josh fought for breath, each one more strained than the last. Anders started to sweat in spite of the raw air. The warrior pointed at the boys and cried out in a language that neither of them understood. Josh quivered as the terror pounded through him, weakening his legs and almost causing him to crumple to the ground. Anders reached out to support him. From deep inside, Anders summoned enough energy to mumble,

'It's him.'

The taste of metal in the air became stronger as the mist thickened and the birds continued their ghostly calls that resounded amongst the ruins. So near. The Viking warrior inched towards the boys who took heavy steps backwards. Josh fumbled for the cross in his pocket but as he did so he stumbled and dropped it on the ground. Even though the mist obscured the sun, the cross started to glow, causing the Viking to halt his advance. He roared again at the boys and swung his sword at them. Then a yell like a battle cry and the words,

'Haraldr Grafeldr! Sigr!'

Josh's breathing grew louder whilst Anders' heart beat so fast that it seemed it would explode inside him. They were so disorientated by the chanting and the dense, swirling haze that they wouldn't have known in what direction to run even if they'd had the strength. Josh made a grab for the gleaming cross but the swooping birds drove him back.

The temperature plunged the closer the warrior came. Ice started to form on the ground. Shivering, Josh tried to rub his arms to stay warm but he couldn't move his hands. So cold. Anders felt no effect of the increasing chill and reached out to Josh who, unaccountably, felt a warmth flow through him. It seemed as if Anders was transferring his own body heat to his friend.

The warrior loomed over them and raised his sword above his head. He was about to strike out at the boys when a great rushing noise boomed from the edge of the abbey grounds. It sounded like the rumbling of an express train. Then the ground began shaking as the din grew louder. An intense blaze pierced the gloom but it came from behind the boys and not just the glowing cross. Josh and Anders were too afraid to look around but saw the effect that it had on Greycloak who took several steps back towards the group of warriors. He shouted out more defiant words but the only one that Josh could recognise was Freyja.

For a while everything stopped. Too scared to move, the boys waited for the worst.

The mist started to separate and the ice began to melt just as the breeze welled up. With a defiant thrust of his sword into the air, Greycloak edged away, followed by the other warriors and the two birds. Daylight seeped through the clouds and the air thawed as the Viking faded away. The choking, metallic air that hung so heavy loosened its grip and a purer, fresher scent, like sunrise, took hold. The storm, which had previously raged above them, unfurled and withdrew across the sea. Slumping on their hands and knees, the boys looked as if all their energy had been drained away. Anders continued looking in the direction of the Vikings as Josh stared at the ground, panting.

'We're OK. It's my friend,' croaked Josh who turned around warily, grasping Anders' arm, to see what caused the noise. He lurched backwards, bringing them both to the ground. Open-jawed and gulping air, they clawed themselves away from the sight in front of them. Standing on the remnants of a crumbling stone column was a being similar in all aspects to the painting of the Shield Maiden Freyja in Nathan's house. Although she had the appearance of a human there was an unearthly quality about her. She wore the same white feather cloak and carried a glimmering shield in the form of a bird wing. Her sun-yellow hair was long. It flowed in the breeze whilst soft white lights danced around her. A gentle shimmer replaced the previous brilliance.

Images of Rachel flashed at intervals through Josh's head as the two boys scrambled to their feet. Smiling, the lady pointed towards the sea. They turned around and saw the storm clouds retreating towards the horizon. When they heard another gushing sound they looked back for her. She had vanished. By the time they spoke, the sun had reclaimed its rightful place in the sky.

'We've got to tell someone,' said Josh.

'Who'd believe us?'

Josh kept looking in all directions to be sure that Greycloak had not reappeared but there was no sign. After a while he said,

'Rachel. Rachel would.'

Then Josh cried out as if something had scared him. He fumbled on the ground.

'What? What?' asked Anders.

Josh ran his hands over the grass and crawled on all fours peering to and fro.

'The cross!'

It had now stopped glowing and nestled in a hollow by a cluster of stone remains. As the sun intensified, a glint of light caught Josh's eye and he scrambled towards it. Letting out a gasp of air, he retrieved the cross, gripped it in clenched fists then lay motionless as Anders crawled beside him.

'How come you didn't feel freezing when Greycloak came?' asked Josh.

Anders shrugged his shoulders and looked away. Josh wondered if there was something his best friend wasn't telling him.

They sat on the ground in silence absorbing the warmth of the sun, trying to understand what they had just witnessed. Normality returned as seagulls squawked, children called out and the smell of the sea took hold. The knots in their stomachs unwound and their senses, heightened by the appearance of the Vikings, started to relax.

'Who was that lady?' asked Anders.

Josh said nothing. His mind spun in all directions and he hadn't heard Anders' words.

'Josh. Josh! Who do you think she was?'

'Eh? Oh…she was…like the painting.'

'What painting?'

'At Nathan's. I found a picture in a book. It said Shield Maiden of the Houses of the White Settlement.'

Anders screwed up his face. Josh thought about Rachel, unclenched his fists and gazed at the cross. Safe.

*

Rupert took Josh's letter to the hospital the following morning. Josh asked if he could go with him but Rupert just kept saying 'Maybe another time.' He wondered if there was a reason why he couldn't see her and when 'another time' might be.

Josh spent the next few days brooding on the experience with Greycloak at the abbey and flitting between Kristjan's, 'The Dracula Experience' and fishing with Anders. The boys talked endlessly about their experience amongst the ruins, which made them uneasy about returning, even though they felt something pulling them back there. Josh was desperate to talk to Rachel but he still had doubts about her reaction.

Days were hot and dry. Summer tasted its strongest as the sweet and sour aromas of the seaside clung in the still air. The two boys spent most of their time together but the holidays were approaching their end and Josh knew that he might not be able to stay in Whitby much longer. Joy at seeing his mum again was overshadowed by the heartbreak of having to leave his new friends. Especially Anders. When ever the idea of being wrenched away from them leapt into his mind he tried to squash it by focussing on another thought. At these times his friend would spring up, brushing against his face to soothe away his anxieties.

Josh remembered that when he left home at the beginning of the holidays, he didn't want to leave. Now, as they were ending, part of him didn't want to go back. Yet he longed to see his mum; for her to be well enough to come and live in Whitby then maybe he wouldn't have to go back. That would be best. *But it won't happen.* Rachel's words echoed back to him. What if she was right and all things were working together for good?

Before summer, Josh's life was predictable. He was heading down a straight road that stretched out eternally before him, unconcerned that everything remained the same. Now, he couldn't see a clear direction. Change had been difficult but he would never have thought that going to stay with his uncle would have opened so many doors; even if some of them revealed the unexpected.

In spite of the uncertainty, Josh sensed that perhaps he was being protected. In the past, he would have fretted but now he was becoming accustomed to change. Almost enjoying it. Why, he didn't know but perhaps it didn't matter. It was just another riddle to add to the others he was trying to solve as he sat on the wall with Rover near the caravan when Rupert drove up at the end of the day.

'Hiya,' said Josh hopping down from the wall. 'Did you give mum my letter? Is she okay? When can I see her?'

'Whoa, soldier. One at a time. First off, yes, I did give her your letter. She loved it.'

Josh grinned and bounced from foot to foot.

'So when can I see her?'

'Fancy fish and chips for tea?' asked Rupert.

Why do adults keep avoiding questions? Josh decided to not let it go. He would bide his time and catch Rupert out when he least expected it.

Rover appeared to understand Rupert mentioning fish and he stood up on the wall in anticipation.

'I'll save you some, Rover,' Josh replied. 'I'll set the table.' He was about to head back to the caravan when Rupert called out.

'Thought we'd eat out. Got something to celebrate. Mina's coming with Anders.'

'Where are we going?'

'The Magpie.'

'Yeees! Yeees!' Josh whooped. He had often seen the queues forming outside the restaurant down by the harbour and longed to see what it was like inside. Only later, when they were inside, did he think to ask what they were celebrating.

*

Mina and Anders were waiting for them by the Magpie entrance. The queue had not yet grown too long but anticipation bubbled in Josh as he talked excitedly with the others. He couldn't keep still, asking what they would eat and if he could choose anything. A group of chattering people came out having finished their meal and a kindly aunt of a waitress dressed in black with a white apron led Josh's group upstairs to a table overlooking the river. The wooden tables were laid out precisely with white napkins, side plates, cutlery and place mats depicting scenes of Whitby. The walls were festooned with photographs and paintings of ships, fish and other nautical items as a warm, homely feeling enveloped them.

The menu had so many types of fish that the boys found it difficult to choose. They had heard of cod, haddock and herring but names like skate, halibut, monkfish and lemon sole were new to them. Anders looked at a television with the various names of fish displaying a tick or a cross against them.

'What's that mean?' he asked pointing at the screen.

'If it's got a cross against it that means they've sold out,' explained Rupert.

Josh laughed when he saw one item on the menu.

'Woof? What's a woof?'

'It's a fish that barks,' said Mina with a serious expression.

'Honest?'

'Yeah. No, not really. It's a name they give to a sort of catfish. It's really good. That's what I'm having. You can try some of mine and see if you like it,' she said.

Josh and Anders tucked into bread and butter, waiting for their meal to arrive.

When the waitress brought their fish, hot, golden and so massive that it overlapped the side of the plate, Josh gazed at it in amazement whilst Anders rubbed his hands together. The green of the mushy peas, the yellow of the lemon wedge and corn coloured chips created a palette of colours on the plate.

Mina and Rupert had already started eating when they noticed Josh still staring at his meal.

'You're allowed to eat it, you know,' said Mina pouring tea for everyone.

'It's perfect,' replied Josh.

'Not too perfect to eat though,' said Rupert. 'I'd better help you with yours. You won't be able to scoff all that.' He pretended to cut some of Josh's fish for himself but Josh protested.

'No, no, I can eat it all.'

'Oohhh. Shame,' said Rupert pretending to be disappointed and eyeing up Anders' plate.

The batter crackled as Josh sliced through it revealing the white fish.

They ate in silence for a while then Josh recalled what Rupert had said earlier.

'What are we celebrating?'

'I've spoken to the police. They've charged Nathan with embezzlement and…'

'What's embezzlement?' Josh interrupted, making a sandwich with some chips that overflowed his plate.

'It's like stealing. Because he forged the will. The police said your grandfather's original will is the proper one and it looks like your mum and me will get some of the inheritance. As well as the house, there was some money but I don't know how much.'

'Does that mean you and mum are rich?'

'Well, not rich. But we do have a share in the house.'

'You won't sell the house, will you? It's important. Mr Symes said.'

'We'll see. Anyway, the best thing is about your mum. You tell him, Mina.'

Mina hesitated, pouring another cup of tea to stretch the moment. She looked at everyone in turn, sighed and sat back in her chair. Then she stared out of the window, grinning.

'How do you fancy seeing your mum again?'

'In hospital? When?'

'That's not the best bit,' Mina continued. 'We've got her booked into a convalescent home just up the road. She's going there the day after tomorrow so she can recover after her operation.'

'Because of the inheritance we can afford to pay for her to be properly cared for,' added Rupert, addressing the quizzical look on his nephew's face. 'As soon as she's moved in we'll go and see her.'

Josh's eyes filled with tears and he brushed them away with his shirtsleeve.

'Ohh, love.' Mina cuddled him.

'Okay, buddy?' asked Rupert leaning over to touch Josh's arm.

Josh nodded. Then it struck him.

'Am I staying here?'

'I wondered when that would dawn on you,' answered Rupert. 'I'm afraid you've got the short straw, though.'

'Pardon?' Josh was making a habit of looking puzzled.

'Looks like you'll have to stay with me. Your mum says it's fine.'

Josh almost knocked the table over as he threw his arms around his uncle sitting opposite.

'And you'll be in the same school as Anders,' continued Rupert.

Anders whooped with joy but Josh, who had previously fought back the tears, now sobbed heartily without embarrassment. Other customers at nearby tables gawped at the commotion but Josh didn't care. The exhilaration of that moment was everything to him. His friend outside jangled the window to reinforce the feeling.

Then a question surged through his mind demanding attention.

'Rupert. Why did you come and meet me in Goathland?'

'I'm not sure. Even when I was waiting for your bus I had doubts. I almost left before it arrived. But when I saw you sitting there...well, the look on your face just convinced me. Sometimes...we can't just stand by and watch...we have to make things better...I guess.'

Rupert watched the tears tracking down Josh's face. He got up, kneeled next to Josh and cradled both arms around him. Anders beamed as Mina held his hand.

'We've done okay haven't we?' said Rupert.

Josh immersed himself in Rupert's embrace.

CHAPTER 17

Can some people read others' thoughts?

As they left the restaurant, with Josh carrying some fish in a bag for Rover, the sun had dropped and was kissing the horizon. The crowds had thinned and walking along the harbour front was effortless. Josh's mind was in a whirl at the changes ahead of him; his mum; school with Anders; staying in Whitby. Then there was Rachel.

Strolling past Ruby's café, Josh recalled the doughnut dare he undertook when he first arrived in Whitby. No more laughter. No more Banjo clowning around or the smell of bacon grilling for Mountain's sandwiches.

'Don't know what we're going to do without that place.' Nobody answered Rupert.

On the cliff top they stopped and enjoyed the evening air cooling their faces after the day's heat. The fishing fleet hugged the pier. Whitby relaxed as a cleaner, crisper atmosphere replaced the daytime smells of ice cream kiosks and food stalls. Mina pointed to a large house further west along the cliff road.

'That's where your mum's going to stay. She'll be able to see the abbey from there.'

'Oh, wow!' replied Josh.

Mina realised Anders was only wearing a T-shirt and trousers.

'Did you forget your jacket, Anders?' she asked.

'I didn't bring one.'

He never feels cold.

Night dulled the sky as the sun finally let go its grip, reducing the abbey to a silhouette. They stopped to watch the shadows of people dancing in the lights that shone up against St Mary's church on the far riverbank. As they watched the giant shadow puppets against the church wall, Josh sensed the presence of something circling above and behind them. Eventually they settled on the arched whalebones.

He recognised the sinister shape of the ravens, arching their wings against the backlight of the street lamps. Then they flew above him for a while, before letting out a piercing cry and vanishing. Josh turned to catch up with the others who had walked on ahead of him. Anders had seen it and watched.

'Did you see that?' asked Josh.

Anders nodded but said nothing. He took hold of Josh's arm and guided him away, glancing back to the dark blankness where the ravens had disappeared.

They strolled down to the pier but Anders said he had to get back home. He thanked Rupert for the meal and ran off, zigzagging down the road shouting excited goodbyes to everyone. Three people were sitting on a bench by the bandstand, staring out across the river. From the songs flowing from one of them, they gathered it was Banjo. The lady sitting in the middle was elbowing him, urging him to stop. The bulk of the third person was unmistakeable.

'We thought that was you up there, Banjo,' called Rupert pointing at the church.

'No way DJ! I'm a smoother groover.'

'You mean there's someone just as daft as you in Whitby?' said Mina.

'What are you all doing down here?' asked Rupert.

'No scoff shop,' replied Banjo.

Rachel didn't say anything at first. She was looking into the distance watching Anders run home along the waterfront.

'My mum's coming to live at the convalescent home over there. Do you want to meet her when she arrives?'

Mountain performed his one arm salute. Banjo sang 'I'll be there, yeah, yeah' to his own tune. Rachel turned back from watching Anders and just said 'Of course, lad.'

Banjo stood up on the bench. 'Hey guys. Want to hear my latest song? It goes…'

'Better take foggy bonce home, Mountain. He's scaring the fish,' said Rachel.

Mountain hauled up the warbling Banjo and slung him over his shoulder. The voice drifted away on the night air as Mountain carried him off in the direction of the bridge and back home.

'Hey, Rachel,' said Rupert. 'We're going to Nathan's house again tomorrow. Could you come?'

'Sure, love. So tell me about your friend,' she asked Josh.

'That's Anders. I wanted you to meet him but he had to get home.'

She appeared lost in thought before turning to Josh and hugging him. Mina and Rupert drifted off to watch the river idle by. Josh seized the opportunity and said,

'Rachel. You know when you said you were looking forward to seeing me when I first arrived? What did you mean?'

*

At Nathan's house the next morning, Rachel looked around the hall, her eyes recording everything. She breathed deeply, as if she was drawing in the very soul of the house. Nobody noticed as she closed her eyes and entered a momentary trance-like state, whispering to herself.

Rupert told Mr and Mrs Symes what the police had said and

that they would still need to sort out what to do with the house. Mrs Symes became flustered again and her face strained with worry. Josh wandered off as Rupert and Mina took Mrs Symes off to the kitchen to make some tea and calm her down, leaving Rachel in the hallway with Mr Symes. The old man stared at her. As he looked into her eyes something awoke in him but he couldn't pinpoint it. He wanted to ask her questions but he stopped and looked away. She saw his manner change and diverted his attention.

'Tell me about the house,' she said.

'Don't know as I should.'

When Rachel told him her beliefs about Josh, he softened and recounted some of the things he had told Josh previously.

'Don't sell this house, lady. More to this place than people think. Whitby's in danger.'

'Not just Whitby.'

Her words startled Mr Symes who stood upright and took a step back. His eyes widened.

'You…you're…' but before he could continue Rachel told him about the cross she had given to Josh. Mr Symes became enthusiastic as he spoke about seeing the birthmark on Josh's neck during their long walk.

'There's some think I'm mad,' he said. 'Even Mrs Symes. She won't hear of such talk.'

Rachel touched his arm and smiled.

Josh returned.

'I found 'The Bergen Prophecy.''

Mr Symes gasped and looked down at the floor. The old man composed himself then spoke in hushed tones.

'There's forces.'

Unseen by Josh, Rachel put her finger over her lips and Mr Symes stopped in mid sentence.

'What forces?' Josh demanded.

'Best check Mrs Symes.'

The old man wiped his brow with the back of his hand. As he trudged towards the kitchen, Josh called after him.

'But what forces?'

Mr Symes turned back to look at Josh then headed to the kitchen. Josh kicked out at thin air.

'Why won't people tell me?'

Rachel turned Josh around to face her then placed her hands on his shoulders.

'Sometimes, lad, you have to let the whole ball of string unravel before you can find the end.'

'What's that mean?'

She held Josh close to her as they walked to the kitchen.

*

A more composed Mrs Symes was taking freshly baked scones from the oven. She bristled when Josh appeared. Mina whispered to the old lady out of his earshot.

'Don't blame Josh. It's not his fault.'

'Wrap yourselves around these, you two. Just out of the oven,' said Rupert. 'Hey, Rachel, you must be famous. There's a painting of you in the dining room,' he joked.

Rachel noticed the anxious expression on Josh's face and put her arm around him.

'Your uncle, eh?' she said.

The heart-warming aroma of fresh baking filled the air and drove out the tension that had boiled up. Rachel led Josh to the table and sat him down. She dolloped thick strawberry jam onto their scones and devoured two with ease whilst Josh sought to keep pace with her. Mrs Symes turned away and mumbled to herself when Josh smiled at her and thanked her for the baking.

Josh pleaded with Rupert again to let Mr and Mrs Symes stay in their living quarters at the side of the main house. Whether it was the homemade scones that made up his mind Josh didn't know but his uncle agreed.

'Heeeyyy yaaaa,' shouted Josh who raised his arm in a Mountain-like salute.

'Oh, lad. You've been spending too much time with the terrible two.' Rachel ruffled Josh's hair playfully then pretended to take the last scone off his plate. Josh winked. She put the scone back, laughing.

Mr Symes thanked Rupert and Mrs Symes dried the corner of her eye with her apron before busying herself about the kitchen, humming gently.

'Mind if I take a quick look around the house?' Rachel asked Rupert.

'Me too,' enthused Josh.

He tried to drag her into the dining room to show her the painting but she sidetracked him by examining the carvings in the wooden panels. Rachel's eyes blazed as she ran her hands over the inscriptions. Josh stopped dead. She appeared to be reading them as her fingers walked over the engravings, mouthing words to herself that he couldn't hear.

'What do they say?'

'They're called runes. A bit like letters. The Vikings used them but these are unusual.' She paused. 'These are protection runes.'

'Uh?'

'The owner carved them to…'

'That's my grandfather,' Josh exclaimed.

'Well, he put them on the wood to guard the house and everyone in it when the day comes. This house is built on sacred land.'

'Mr Symes told me the house was special. And I can hear talking… but it's like…friendly. Come on, I'll show you the painting,' said Josh grasping Rachel's arm.

Then he stopped. 'When what day comes?'

She held back, her eyes shining in a way that Josh had never seen before. As she drew Josh close to her, cupping his head in her hands, Josh felt himself sink into a deep peace. He wanted to tell her about the encounter with Greycloak in the abbey. There was no need. It was as if his thoughts were flooding through Rachel's hands and he was telling her without speaking. Rachel held Josh for a while then dropped her hands. Unseen, Mina observed them from a distance.

'Rachel. Can I tell you something?'

'You already have, love,' she said in a soft voice.

*

Mrs Symes continued with her chores but Mr Symes looked nervous as he watched everyone leave. Rachel saw the anxiety in the old man's eyes.

'Don't worry. We're not alone.'

Mina's car clattered away and Rachel rode off, her motorbike belching black smoke from the exhaust. Rupert's motorbike followed with Josh holding onto him. Memories of the night he had left the house swept through his head; skulking through the dark with Mr Symes, worried about his future. As his friend raced with them along the roads back to town, fear gave way to hope. Previously, he never wanted to see that house again. Now, things were different. Nathan had gone and the frosty atmosphere had thawed. In spite of this, one idea wouldn't let go.

There's something weird about this house.

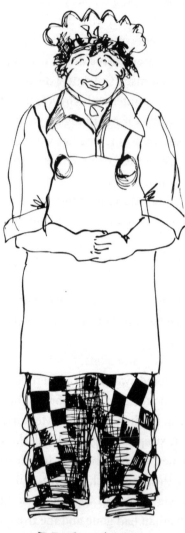

Kristjan

CHAPTER 18

Do words always mean what they say?

A week before Josh was due to start his new school, his mum arrived at the convalescent home on the West Cliff at Whitby. The excitement of being with her and introducing her to his new friends had given him a sleepless night. He had so much to tell her. *Is she really better now?*

Stomach churning, mind spinning, Josh held onto Rachel as they rode on her motorbike along the cliff top road to visit his mum. Whenever Rachel was close he felt at peace. With her there was never a problem that couldn't be overcome. Like his mum, Rachel was comfort in chaos, defence in distress. He was thankful for her. Especially now.

Anders arrived at the home on the back of Mountain's motorbike, followed shortly by Banjo. Rachel had to stop Josh leaping from the bike before it stopped. Staff raised their eyebrows when the leather clad group arrived at the reception desk. Mountain towered above everybody but Josh and Anders led the way, wrestling with helmets that made their heads look bigger than they were.

'I'm Josh Haxby. Can we see my mum please?'

'Oh…yes,' said the receptionist with relief. 'Your uncle came in earlier with another lady. He mentioned you'd be coming,' she continued, still casting a wary look at the group.

Rachel looked at Banjo.

'See, Banjo, you're frightening people. Should've left you outside.'

Banjo pulled a face and poked his tongue out at her behind her back.

'I saw that,' she said.

It was only when Anders removed his helmet that Rachel saw him properly for the first time. She had barely glimpsed him before, disappearing in the half-light on the pier that evening. Now, in the full light streaming through the window, she saw him clearly. Gazing at him, Rachel looked as if she had found a long lost friend. Nobody else spotted it.

The receptionist, a young woman with her hair in a pony tail and dressed in a crisp, white blouse and dark purple skirt, led Josh's group to the lounge. Several residents eyed them uneasily. Josh's mum was sitting in the bay window looking out across the garden. As Josh approached her, Rachel held the others back to give him some time alone with his mum.

He crept up behind his mum and placed his hands over her eyes.

'Guess who?' Then he leapt round and flung his arms around her. She gasped and held him tight, her eyes glistening. They stayed entwined for several minutes. No words were spoken; just holding each other close was all they needed and Josh didn't want to let go in a hurry. His mum straightened his hair and sweatshirt as they gazed at each other.

Josh introduced his friends.

'This is Anders my new best friend. That's Mountain. He saved me from two men and he eats anything. And Banjo. He rescued me from the sea.' He paused before making his final introduction. He lowered his voice to a more respectful tone.

'This is Rachel. She helps me when I don't understand things. She's brilliant.'

Rachel stooped down and held his mum's hands between her own. She looked at Rachel as if they had met before but the moment passed when Banjo broke into song making everyone laugh.

'I got your letter, Josh. It was wonderful to hear from you. Cheered me up no end. Did you get my card?'

Josh nodded.

'Rupert came in earlier and told me everything. I'm so sorry I made you stay with Nathan. I didn't realise.'

Josh squeezed his mum tight then told her everything that happened. She asked countless questions and when Josh couldn't explain anything Rachel helped him out. The others sat patiently close by.

'I'm so grateful you've got such lovely friends. Thank you, all of you, for being there for him.'

'Better let your mum rest eh? You can see her whenever you want now,' said Rachel.

'I'll come in every day, mum.'

'That would be lovely. And your friends as well, I hope. I may have to stay here for a while but the doctors say I'm doing fine.'

Anders, Banjo and Mountain said goodbye leaving Rachel with Josh and his mum.

'He's special your lad,' said Rachel.

'I know. He's a lovely boy.'

'More than that. There's a reason for him being in Whitby. He must never leave unless fate tells him to.'

'I…I don't understand.'

'It's a lot to take in but…trust me. Anything you need, let me know.'

'Thank you for looking after Josh. You've been really kind.'

Josh kissed his mum and gave her a last hug.

'See you later, mum.'

'Bye, Josh. Love you.'

He wiped some tears with his shirtsleeve and waved to his mum as he left with Rachel.

They searched for the others but couldn't see them, either in reception or with the motorbikes. Rachel was about to ask one of the staff when they heard a piano playing and Banjo singing. Walking towards the music, they entered a welcoming, green painted, high ceilinged room where a number of people were gathered around Banjo who enthusiastically hammered out a tune. Anders pretended to conduct the singing as Josh and Rachel grinned at the antics of their friends.

'Got to have an audience that Banjo,' said Rachel.

'I didn't know he could play piano.'

'Plays anything, him. Usually the fool.'

They couldn't see Mountain in the group so Rachel went to ask the receptionist.

'Not seen a big bloke in a leather jacket?' asked Rachel.

'Yes. He's taking some patients around the garden.'

'Some…right. Thanks, love.'

Josh followed Rachel outside where they saw Mountain pushing two people side by side in wheelchairs so that they could talk to each other on their trip around the grounds. Many people would have struggled to push even one wheelchair around but Mountain made it look easy. He nodded and grinned as the two patients chatted and joked together pointing out flowers and shrubs in the garden.

'Does nothing by halves does he?' said Rachel.

Josh noticed the two large ravens perched on the front gate of the home. Watching. Rachel sensed his nervousness and placed her arm around his shoulder.

'They keep following me,' he said.

She replied in a voice that gave no hint of anxiety. As if everything was normal.

'The Vikings call them the brow stars of Loki, the fire god.' Josh gave her a vacant look. 'Try and work it out,' she continued.

Josh groaned but didn't notice that she spoke of Vikings as if they still existed.

Anders joined them as the ravens flew silently away. The three sat on a bench chatting in the warming sun, waiting for Banjo and Mountain to return.

'Did you see them?' whispered Anders to Josh who nodded and turned towards him.

'She already knew about Greycloak,' he said.

Rachel smiled at them both.

'Didn't I say it'd work out okay?' said Rachel nudging Josh.

'I've still got your note,' he replied, pulling out the crumpled piece of paper from his trouser pocket.

'Decided who you're going to share that cross with?' continued Rachel glancing at Anders.

'It's going to be…'

Josh couldn't finish his sentence. A thick, strong arm wrapped around him from behind and shook him playfully. Josh heard the familiar growl and sniggered.

Banjo joined them on the bench shortly after.

'Come on,' Rachel said to Josh. 'The dopey duo are back.'

'Hey, I heard that,' complained Banjo.

'I still love you,' said Josh.

'Big up to you, Joshy boy.'

Mountain lifted up Banjo and Anders in a bear hug and carried them back to the motorbikes. Rachel and Josh followed, waving at Josh's mum in the window.

*

The three motorbikes drove down the Khyber Pass that snaked below the crossed whalebones towards the harbour. They noticed Rupert and Mina walking up the hill towards them. It was lunchtime and the streets were thronging with crowds, now swollen with workers enjoying a break under the canopy of a cornflower blue sky. Rachel pulled alongside them followed by the others.

'Hey! How did it go with your mum?' asked Rupert.

'It was brilliant. I'm going back every day.'

'Where you two headed?' asked Rachel.

'Thought we might get a bite to eat.'

'I know where we could go,' enthused Anders almost falling off the back of Mountain's motorbike.

'My dad's restaurant. You'll love it. He makes fantastic krumkake.'

'Yeah! Let's get some crummy cake!' yelled Banjo.

Anders gave directions to Kristjan's and the motorbikes purred away with Rupert and Mina following on foot.

Josh still couldn't get the protection runes off his mind.

*

Kristjan stood in the restaurant, arms folded behind him with his laundry white apron neatly tied around his waist. He was peering hopefully through the window for customers when three motorbikes pulled up outside. Kristjan retreated to the back of the restaurant at the sound of the smoking machines and the appearance of the faceless invaders. Mountain, still wearing his leathers and crash helmet, stood in the doorway, blocking out some of the light. He stood still as Banjo jostled him from behind trying to get in.

Kristjan reached for the telephone, his anxiety rising. Anders crawled through Mountain's legs, removed his helmet and beamed up at his dad whose jaw dropped.

'Hi, pappa. Look, new customers.'

'Oh! It you, my boy.' Kristjan wiped his forehead and replaced the phone. 'Good, good. Welcome everyone. Welcome.'

Although still in a state of disbelief, he regathered his composure and ushered everyone to the best tables.

'I have food ready. Plenty.'

'These are our friends,' Anders announced, introducing everyone.

'You friends of Anders and Josh, now you my friends.'

Banjo looked around for something to eat. 'Hey, what's to eat? I could scoff a skunk.'

'Not have skunk. Have lapskaus. Good stew, fresh,' explained Kristjan.

'And krumkake,' said Josh.

'Always krumkake. You hungry, big guy?' said Kristjan, marvelling at the size of Mountain who grinned expectantly.

Kristjan went to the kitchen but soon returned with a huge tray of savoury and sweet dishes that everyone devoured almost without stopping. Rupert and Mina arrived later. Kristjan, a broad smile stretching across his face, showed them to a table by the window with a view of the river then brought over their food.

Standing in the middle of his restaurant, Kristjan roared with laughter at the picture of satisfaction that he had created.

'You'll never get rid of us now,' said Rupert.

'Like our very own munch mansion,' added Banjo.

Mountain gave a stifled version of his regular salute and almost poked Banjo in the eye with a chunk of bread.

'Maybe I get help in restaurant now,' said Kristjan.

'I know,' yelled Josh. 'Ruby! She could help.'

'Good call, lad,' said Rachel. 'I'll call her later if you like?'

'Yes, good, good. She start tomorrow.'

Anders and Josh sidled off to another table to talk.

'How come she already knew about Greycloak in the abbey?'

'Don't know,' replied Josh fiddling with a paper napkin on the table.

Josh turned and smiled at Rachel who joined them in the corner away from the crowd.

Banjo noticed a guitar propped against the wall and started entertaining everyone with folk songs that carried through the open door to the street. The sounds attracted more customers. Kristjan welcomed them in his typically bubbly way.

'I give you job, Banjo. You bring customers.'

The restaurant's earlier emptiness changed into a more homely feel that wrapped itself around everybody like a comforting blanket. The place had found its spirit.

Rupert joined Banjo in leading the singing whilst Mina watched Rachel and the boys from her table. As Rachel spoke to Anders his face contorted with confusion but Josh listened attentively, nodding encouragement to him every so often. Mina didn't know what they were discussing but when Josh took the cross out and Rachel covered the boys' hands over it with her hand she watched more intently. She waited for the right time to join them.

As they talked, the questions kept swirling in Josh's head. He still couldn't explain why Rupert had taken him to Whitby or how Banjo managed to save him, especially when he couldn't swim. And that lady on the cliff top? What were the chances of meeting Anders and him being from Greycloak's hometown? How did Rachel know so much about Josh's and Anders' futures? Why did she continually remind him of the painting of Freyja the Shield Maiden? Then there was 'The Bergen Prophecy.' Was it real? Maybe Rachel and Mr Symes had it all wrong.

Josh took out the loose page of kennings and showed it again to Rachel.

'You said October before. Where does it say that?' asked Josh.

Rachel took a deep breath before replying, then pointed to the words on the sheet.

'Where it says manuor of gor, that means the month of October in Norse. The language of the Vikings.'

'So something's going to happen on the twenty first of October. What this year?' asked Anders. But Rachel didn't get the chance to reply.

'And the white settlement's Whitby isn't it?' added Josh.

Anders studied the kennings again, like a master detective trying to unravel clues about a crime. Rachel looked on.

'It's like a puzzle,' said Anders. 'What if they use more words than they need to?...then maybe...sail is something about ships...a road for ships is...'

'Sea!' exclaimed Josh. 'So what are storm steeds? I know a steed's a horse. Mrs Cooper read it from a book about the Romans. Sam thought it was a bike but we all laughed.'

Anders was in stitches at the idea of Romans riding around on bikes and Rachel lifted a hand to her mouth to stop giggling. Anders examined the kenning again.

'This part about a storm...that could be...thunder, lightning... rain.' He thought a while longer. 'And they ride on clouds.'

Rachel sat back in her chair and gazed in approval like a mother bird watching her young learn to fly for the first time. Josh screwed up his face as he studied the words.

'But what about the fatherless one?'

The moment was broken as Mina joined them. She didn't say anything. Instead, she took their hands and held them together in the middle of the table, gazing at each of them in turn. Her eyes rested on Rachel who looked at her in an understanding way. Then she kissed them goodbye, thanked Kristjan and left the restaurant with Rupert. Josh watched Mina leave. *Does she know something?*

Banjo continued entertaining the customers who now filled the restaurant apart from one vacant table. Mountain just kept eating.

'How come you know everything, Rachel?' asked Anders.

Rachel hugged him but didn't answer.

'Did you know I'd show the cross to Anders?' said Josh with a bemused look.

Grinning, Rachel nudged him.

'It's like my birthmark. Look.'

Josh rolled down the collar of his shirt. Anders looked at his neck.

'What?'

'There, look,' said Josh pointing.

'I can't see anything.'

'But…' He went over to the mirror on the wall behind the till to check for himself. Nothing.

'I've had that mark since I was born.'

'You don't need it now you've got the cross,' said Rachel. 'Let's go up to St Mary's church. Something I want to show you.'

Anders told his dad who, by now, was performing his own dance routine to Banjo's music. Kristjan kissed Rachel's hand whilst Josh pawed at his neck, shaken by the uncanny disappearance of his birthmark.

Rainbow

CHAPTER 19

If you knew the future, how would you feel?

Rachel, with the boys on either side of her, strolled along the riverside towards the bridge. A tall masted yacht kept pace with them but they had to wait when the bridge swung to the side to release the boat to the vastness of the North Sea. It was a sight Josh had seen many times and he still saw himself as a boat leaving harbour. A voyage that began when he first left home that morning with Mrs Kendrick.

Three seagulls flew above the yacht escorting it past the lifeboat station. At a nearby stall, Rachel bought a large bag of marshmallows that they chewed during their wait for the bridge to swing back in place. They competed with each other to see how long they could keep the soft, spongy sweetness in their mouths before chewing. Josh had no discipline when it came to eating sweets slowly and quickly gave in.

'You may be the doughnut demon but Anders is the marshmallow marvel,' said Rachel casting an eye towards the harbour entrance and the sea.

Waiting for the bridge to move back, Anders leaned against some railings and watched a group of nosey pigeons waddling in his direction to investigate the bag of marshmallows. Rachel glanced around as if she was looking for someone or something. Then she stared at the pier that was now shrouded by mist.

Josh remembered.

'I think I've worked it out! Brow stars.'

'Go on then,' encouraged Rachel.

'Well, brows could be eyebrows. And stars are bright and they shine. So the stars of eyebrows could be …eyes? The ravens are like eyes?'

Rachel winked at Josh who glowed with satisfaction at working out the riddle. But his face changed when he realised the implications of his discovery. Ravens. Eyes. Watching. Rachel saw the recognition sweeping across his face but the churning mist rolling over the water towards the bridge distracted them.

When the bridge swivelled back into place and the barriers were raised, people started to cross over and cars edged forwards. Josh and Rachel kept watching the mist as they followed Anders who was more concerned with the remains of his marshmallows. As they approached the middle, the bridge began to swing back to the side without reason. Two women escorting a group of lively, clamouring children across the bridge were walking backwards to the widening gap as they tried to keep everyone together.

A small boy climbed onto the side of the bridge and one of the women rushed to stop him as the other children became excited. None of the group was aware that the bridge had reopened. Josh and Anders felt a breath on their faces. They turned to see them heading towards the opening with the risk that somebody would tumble into the river.

'Stop! Stop!' Josh yelled but they didn't hear him above the din. Other people called out. Only when a young girl, similar in age to the boys, ran from nowhere and grasped the arm of one of the women did she realise what was happening. She shouted out to her colleague and together they shepherded the youngsters to safety. Josh and Anders ran up to help.

'Thank you so much,' said one of the women to the young girl. 'We didn't notice with all the racket.'

'I can't understand it. That's never happened before,' said the bridge keeper anxiously checking that nobody was hurt.

Other people ran up to lend a hand whilst the bridge closed back into place. An official looking man, with the help of a policeman, shouted out instructions to everyone and organised their safe crossing. The two women watched hawk-like over the children as they followed the crowds over the bridge.

'Wow! I've never seen anyone run that fast,' said Anders to the young girl.

'It's like you came from nowhere. I'm Josh and this is my best friend Anders.'

'I'm Hilda. But some people call me Rainbow,' she replied.

Josh and Anders gave her a puzzled look when she mentioned two names but their concentration was broken when she started examining a tear on the white swan pattern on her purple tee shirt.

'Will your mum be mad with you?' asked Josh.

'I live with my auntie. She's used to me doing this but she'll fix it…oh, is this yours?'

Hilda stooped down and picked up Josh's cross and chain which he had dropped as he ran up to help the children. He smiled, thanked her and then remembered what Rachel had said about only letting two other people hold the cross.

Rachel watched them from a distance then turned and looked out towards the pier where the swirling fog retreated back across the sea. As she stared towards the horizon, Hilda and the boys looked up at two ravens flying at speed in the direction of the dwindling gloom. Following their line of flight they saw Rachel.

'What's she staring at?' asked Anders.

Josh didn't reply.

Hilda walked over to Rachel and started talking to her. They spent a while chatting as the boys mooched around, baffled as to what was keeping them. Anders tapped his shoes against the bridge's railings and peered over the edge at some tree branches drifting downriver to the sea. Josh fiddled with his cross and chain. When they glanced up again, Rachel and Hilda were walking back towards them.

'Is it all right if Rainbow joins us?' asked Rachel.

The boys nodded although they weren't sure why Rachel had suggested it or why she called her Rainbow and not Hilda.

The four of them crossed the bridge turning left up Church Street towards the one hundred and ninety nine steps and St Mary's church. Smoke from Fortune's kipper shop wafted over them as they started to climb the steps whilst the blare from the steam bus, Old Glory, drifted from the other side of the river. Hilda rushed into a shop selling trinkets and souvenirs.

'I'll just tell auntie where I'm going,' she said. 'It's her shop. I'll catch you up.'

At the top of the steps Rachel and the boys walked through the churchyard where huddles of people were inspecting moss encrusted gravestones, eroded by the wind and sea air. Hilda caught up with them but, unlike the others, didn't seem out of breath after her climb. Josh and Anders were surprised again that she managed to join them so quickly.

'Over there. Should get a good view.' Rachel led them to a bench looking out to sea. The yacht they saw previously had raised its mainsail and was heading east towards open water. Josh and Anders settled either side of her as Hilda sat on the grass in front of them.

Josh played with his cross and chain.

'It's nice. Glad you didn't lose it,' said Hilda.

'I dropped it on the bridge but Hilda found it for me,' explained Josh turning to Rachel.

The look on Rachel's face suggested she knew what he was thinking.

'Do you think it would be okay to share the cross with Hilda as well as Anders?' he asked her.

Rachel didn't say anything. There was no need. She put her arm around him and kissed him on the top of his head. That was the only confirmation he needed. Then she kissed Anders and held out her hand to Hilda.

'Do you and Hilda know each other?' asked Anders.

'I've known her since…well, for a long time,' replied Rachel.

Hilda gave her an inquiring look.

'What did you want to show us?' Anders continued.

'See those clouds to the north west?' said Rachel, pointing. 'Like horses' tails. Then some other clouds. Lower and thicker. Look like mackerel skins don't they? Soon, there'll be a storm.'

'Why are you telling us this?' queried Josh.

'To protect you.'

Hilda nodded as if she had heard it before but the boys' faces turned a worried shade of pale. Rachel saw their reaction and put a reassuring arm around both of them. They leaned into her and gazed at the harbour entrance where a pleasure boat eased its way between the two piers with its cargo of holidaymakers. She continued to clasp them tight.

'There are signs in the weather,' added Rachel. 'Learn to read them and they'll guide you.'

'It's true. My auntie told me and she's really clever,' said Hilda.

'Remember a while ago when we had that sudden storm roll in?' Rachel continued.

Josh and Anders sat bolt upright and looked at each other. Rachel waited in case they said anything but they just fidgeted on the bench. Hilda narrowed her eyes and focused on the boys as if she was looking deep inside them.

'That morning,' Rachel continued, 'the clouds came across the sea from the north. Just a few at first. Then more, until they all joined together in a flat layer. Horizontal and hanging over the town. They were harm-bringers but they're not the worst.'

The boys frowned and Josh was on the brink of speaking when Anders said,

'How do you know they were these…?'

'Harm-bringers? Several things. Shape, colour, and direction they were moving. The ones shaped like anvils are the worst. I saw the storm close in.'

Josh spun round abruptly towards Rachel as a tumbling sensation rolled through his stomach.

Rachel sat back on the bench and composed herself.

'The man you saw in the abbey. You know that was Harald Greycloak don't you?' she said.

'But how did you know…you weren't…?' Anders mumbled.

Rachel didn't answer him directly but continued her explanation. Josh looked at Anders. They were thinking the same thing.

'Greycloak was from Bergen.'

'That's where I lived in Norway!'

Rachel smiled, stroked Anders' cheek and carried on.

'Over a thousand years ago, Eric Bloodaxe came from Bergen with his son, Harald Greycloak, and many Viking warriors. Fierce men they were. They conquered the land and Bloodaxe became king. They treated everyone harshly but the people rose up against them, killing the king. Greycloak escaped and returned to Bergen. Because Whitby was the last place he stood on English ground it was against Whitby he vowed to take his revenge first.'

'Where was he king?' asked Anders.

'He was king of Jorvik,' said Rachel.

'That's York isn't it? I've been to the museum!' Josh shouted. 'They said there were only four ghosts but I saw five! And it was him in my garden!'

'He was watching you,' added Rachel. 'Waiting for the right time.'

'The right time for what?' asked Josh.

Before she could reply Anders dived in with a question.

'The man we saw in Bergen. Was that…?'

Rachel took hold of his hand again as his body tightened. She explained that 'The Bergen Prophecy' was written as a coded warning about how and when Greycloak would take his revenge. Anders was about to ask another question but Josh got his in first.

'The Prophecy said someone whose name is deliverer. Who's that?'

Even though he thought he knew the answer, Josh had to ask anyway.

Rachel turned to Hilda inviting her to reply.

'That's you. Josh means deliverer,' said Hilda.

Josh slipped the cross and chain over his head and placed it around his neck, looking for reassurance. The breeze welled up and engulfed the four of them in a warm swirl.

'You were chosen,' said Rachel, 'but you need Anders and Rainbow to help you. I had to wait until your destinies brought you together before I could be sure.'

'You'll be with us though, won't you?' asked Anders.

'Of course I will.'

The more Rachel said, the more questions the boys asked. Hilda said nothing but listened as if she was recording every word. She seemed untroubled by the revelations.

The boys edged closer to Rachel whilst Hilda rested her head on Rachel's knee as they all sat staring out at the bustling town and sea spread out before them. *Greycloak can't destroy all these people.* The more Josh thought about them the more determined he became to do everything he could to protect them. But what power did he have against a Viking warrior and his phantom hordes?

Rachel sensed what Josh was thinking.

'You know, Josh, if you ever get worried and your mum isn't

there to talk to?' He nodded. 'What would you do?'

Josh thought for a while and gazed out to sea.

'It's like…hard to describe…but I know my friend will always be there. Like having a dad as well I suppose. Except I haven't got one.'

He looked down at the ground. Rachel leaned towards him and brushed her cheek against his face. Anders noticed the pained look on Josh's face.

'Isn't it weird that I haven't got a mum and you haven't got a dad?'

'And I haven't got either,' added Hilda. 'But my auntie's great.'

Rachel was about to say something but she stopped herself and just gazed at the young girl tenderly.

Josh looked up, forced a smile and continued. He described how the breeze emerged from nowhere and comforted him even though he couldn't see it. When it spoke it didn't use words. Just a touch was all that he needed to understand. Then, when it had brought calm and hope, it vanished, leaving no sign of where it had gone.

'It's like I know what it's saying,' Josh added, shuffling uneasily, afraid that everyone would think he was crazy.

'That's your gift, love,' Rachel reassured him. 'Listen to what he says.'

'He?'

The others hung onto her next words.

'Tell us,' urged Anders tugging at her arm.

'I could but you have to find the answer yourselves. I'll help you but you've got to make the journey.'

Rachel saw the baffled expression on Josh's face.

'What is it love?' she asked.

'My granddad. He knew about the breeze didn't he? That's why he gave me the wind chime when I was a baby.'

'You got there.'

Josh's words encouraged Anders to say what he had never told anyone before. Not even his best friend.

'Can I tell you something?' asked Anders.

Josh looked baffled. Rachel nodded and Hilda sat closer in expectation.

'I never feel cold. Even in winter.'

'Ohhhh, is that all?' asked Hilda.

'No.'

'Go on, tell us.'

He fidgeted as he told how he was born in a snowstorm. His mother had been left alone in the deep cold because his father was working away. The blizzard stopped him getting back home. When he arrived back two days later, he found his wife dead but Anders was still alive as if someone had been caring for him. Yet there was no sign of anyone having been in the house.

'Really? Nobody else was there?' asked Josh.

Anders shook his head then said,

'They thought my dad made it up but he didn't. Ever since then it's like I can make heat.'

'Is that why I stopped shivering when you touched my arm in the abbey?' asked Josh.

'Mmm.'

'Wow! I wish I was like that,' said Hilda. 'I get cold just getting out of the shower. But then my auntie makes me hot chocolate and I'm all right.'

She hunched her shoulders and giggled.

Nobody spoke for a while. They were trying to take everything in. Apart from Rachel who gave the impression that she had known all this for some time. Yet there was more she needed to tell them. She waited as Josh grappled with another question popping in his head.

'Why do things keep happening when I'm around?' he asked. 'Like on the bridge just now. And the pushchair on the steps.'

'They're signs. Of times to come. But things have always worked out, haven't they?'

Josh took out Rachel's note and nodded at her.

'But what times?' Anders wanted more information but Rachel kept her peace and gave him one of her teasing smiles.

Josh lazed back on the grass, cloud watching. Anders closed his eyes and held his face to the sun. He looked as if he was absorbing the rays, preparing himself for the next time he would need to fight the cold. Hilda picked a flat blade of grass and placed it between her thumbs. When she blew on it, she made a whistling sound which made Anders chuckle but Josh was still cloud dreaming. She picked some more grass and tossed it in the air so it landed on Josh's nose tickling him, prompting him to ask,

'Hilda?'

'Call me Rainbow. It's what my auntie calls me.'

'Oh…okay. How did you get to be such a quick runner?'

She swung round to face Rachel who winked at her. Rainbow told them that four years ago, a cheetah cub bit her on a school trip to a safari park.

'But it didn't hurt. There wasn't even any blood. Just a couple of small fang marks.'

She showed the boys the two neat scars on the back of her hand.

'Since then I've always been able to run quickly. They even stopped me entering school sports day. It was so unfair. It was the only thing I ever won.'

Rolling over on his stomach, Josh looked at her with scrunched up eyes and a blank expression.

'Why do people call you Rainbow?' asked Anders turning away from the sun and opening his eyes.

'I hear everything in colour,' she said.

'Uh?' Josh grunted.

'Mm. When somebody speaks I see colours. Sounds as well.'

'What every word?' Anders continued.

'Most.'

She picked more grass and rolled it in her hands.

'The words sort of...stand out in front of me in bright colours.'

Josh asked what the colours were for 'Why haven't you done your homework?' Anders sniggered. Rainbow continued.

'Haven't is orangey red. Home is white and work is brown. The others are a bit mixed up.'

Anders said it must be like having a kaleidoscope spinning in your head.

'Sometimes it's like fireworks,' she said. 'But it helps me work out if things are true. When the colours are all wavy then I know something's not right. The colours are a sort of warning. Wavy deep red is worst. Like danger.'

Josh and Anders screwed up their noses and stared at her but Rachel caressed her face and looked on her with soft eyes. Rainbow paused and looked at the others, unsure about what they would think of her. Anders stood up and kicked the dead heads off dandelions strewn on the grass.

'Why do boys always kick things like they're playing football?' asked Rainbow.

Rachel laughed.

'When you said you had to wait until our destinies brought us together,' said Josh, 'was it because we've all got these creepy...?'

'Gifts,' said Rachel. 'They're special not creepy. You are the one, like Mr Symes told you, but you need Anders and Rainbow with you. Together, your powers are the only way to prevent Greycloak destroying everything.'

Anders stopped kicking dandelions and did a forward roll, crashing into Josh and Rainbow who chuckled.

Rachel cupped Josh's face in both her hands, as if she was channelling energy through them. Then she did the same with Anders and Rainbow.

'Everything's been working towards this. All three of you were chosen to be here but it wasn't until Rainbow picked up the cross on the bridge that I knew I had my third Principality.'

'Princi what?' Josh spluttered.

'Principality. That's what you three are. It's the name given by The Lord to the seventh order of holiness.'

Anders, for once, kept still then asked,

'What does it mean? And who's The Lord.'

Rachel sat back on the bench, composed herself then settled back to tell the story she had waited so long to reveal. Sounds from the harbour and beach faded, the breeze rested and clouds paused in the sky. Creation held its breath as Rachel began.

'There's too much to tell you everything and I'm only allowed to show you certain truths now. But this I can reveal.'

As she continued an aura surrounded her, gleaming in an unworldly but calming way.

'You were chosen by The Lord for good and to defeat the forces of destruction. Greycloak is one of those forces but he has others who he will summon, stronger and more powerful even than him. This is your calling but you won't be alone.'

Josh, Anders and Rainbow looked at each other.

She waited to allow her words to sink in. They had so many questions, which got in each other's way in the rush to get out of their heads. Josh and Anders looked at each other, then at Rainbow who raised her eyebrows and half smiled at them.

'Did you already know?' Anders asked her.

'My auntie sort of said.'

Josh slumped back on the grass but Anders shadow duelled with a make believe sword. Creation breathed again. Sounds rose up from the town and clouds continued their trek across the sky. The breeze wafted around them playing with their hair and engulfing them in a balmy mixture of sun, sea and grass.

One question clambered above the others wrestling in Josh's head.

'So what do the protection runes at the house mean?'

'The house is a shelter from Greycloak,' said Rachel. 'Your grandfather understood the Prophecy when he built it. That's why he put the runes there. Mr Symes was right about your mum and her brothers being sent away for their safety but your grandfather knew you'd come back. It's in the Prophecy.'

Josh looked directly into Rachel's eyes then confided,

'When I was there it felt…will you think I'm mad if I tell you?'

'Yeah,' Anders joked.

Josh smiled and Rachel touched his hand to reassure him.

'It was like someone was trying to speak to me. But I couldn't hear them properly.'

Rachel held his shoulders with both hands.

'Your grandfather's energy is still in the house. Listen. He'll help you.'

'Hey! A talking house. I can't wait,' enthused Rainbow.

In spite of her fateful words, Anders and Rainbow played with white dandelion seed heads that floated in the breeze. Josh turned everything over in his mind. If Rachel and his granddad were on their side and The Lord, who ever that was, had chosen them, did it matter who was against them? His friends were with him and his mum was nearby. Everything was in place. The beginning.

Josh took a deep breath.

'He's coming back isn't he?'

Rachel didn't answer. She looked out to sea then back to Josh.

'If the ravens are the brow stars of Loki, then who's Loki and what's he got to do with Greycloak?' Josh continued.

'Bet they're working together,' said Anders punching an imaginary enemy.

Turning to him, Rachel gave Anders a look that confirmed his words and said,

'The prophecy says that Greycloak will call upon Loki the fire god and his evil sons to help him in his wickedness.'

'Who are his sons?' asked Josh.

'Aren't they…?' Rainbow was about to say but Rachel looked at her and with a tilt of her head stopped her from revealing anything more. Turning to Josh and Anders in turn, Rachel fixed them with her eyes, burning deep into their minds and erasing particular questions that she didn't want them to ask.

The spell of silence was broken only when a seagull landed nearby, squawked and toddled towards them. It stopped, looked at them like they were some bizarre creatures in a zoo, then moved on to investigate two elderly ladies sitting on another bench eating ice cream. Anders and Rainbow laughed at it but Josh was watching Rachel.

'How old are you, Rachel?' he asked.

'Oh…quite young really. Only a thousand years old,' she teased.

But Josh wasn't convinced she was joking.

'My auntie says that,' added Rainbow.

Images of the painting at Nathan's house flashed again through Josh's mind. One question refused to be ignored.

'Who are you really?'

Rachel shook her head and waited before replying.

'There's a question, lad.'

Josh looked down at the cross and chain, toying with it nervously. Rainbow leaned forward and wrapped his hands in hers. Anders joined in briefly then got up to lie in the sun next to a blue butterfly with grey tinged wings that was lazing in the heat. The breeze skipped around them, wafting in fragrances of just-cut hay from the fields behind the abbey. Deep in thought, Josh stared across the North Sea, his eyes set on the far horizon. He narrowed his eyes as if he was focusing on a blurred object.

Rachel studied him.

'You can see them, can't you?' she said.

Josh didn't need to reply. Even though Rainbow couldn't see the spectre of dragon headed longships that Josh saw on the skyline, she became aware of a change in Josh.

'My auntie says worrying won't make it better or help you live longer. So I just eat strawberry liquorice if I get upset. Anybody want some?' she asked, producing a scrunched up paper bag from her jeans pocket.

Anders sat up and scrambled over to Rainbow.

'Let them come. We're ready,' he mumbled, chewing on the sticky sweetness.

The butterfly didn't move as if it was giving support.

'Are we going to be all right, Rachel?' asked Josh.

'Of course, love. Now we're together,' she replied, standing up.

She nodded in the direction of a pink and yellow van in the car park.

'Right! Who wants ice cream?'

Thank you from the author

I have many people to thank for their help. From the first steps, when Jannah gave me her considerable help, to my family and writing partners for their editing and encouragement. My thanks also goes to those in a well known chain of coffee shops whose patience and constant supply of coffee and granola bars sustained me.

My family: Micheline, Faye, Alex and Nicky.

My writing partners: Owen, Ian, Mary, Sylvia, Paddy, Annie, Beth.

My sustainers: Karen, Jill, Veronica, Elliot, Sam, Jonny, Gemma, Jess, Hannah, Molly, Suzanne, Simon, Helen, Joanna. (and others I'm sure)

My primary school helpers: Ella, Emily, Charlie.

Thanks also to Jenny, Sandra at The Bowery and the staff at Troubador.

And a massive 'thank you' to Dawn for all the illustrations that have added so much to the story and given it a whole new dimension.

Back cover ravens images provided under Creative Commons

To God be the glory

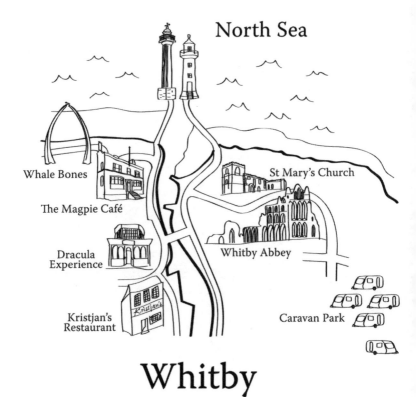

North Sea

Whale Bones

The Magpie Café

Dracula
Experience

Kristjan's
Restaurant

St Mary's Church

Whitby Abbey

Caravan Park

Whitby

To everyone who wants to be loved.